ISABELLA PANFIDO

VENICE NOIR:
THE DARK HISTORY OF THE LAGOONS

translated by Christine Donougher

Dedalus

This book has been translated thanks to a translation grant awarded by the Italian Ministry of Foreign Affairs and International Cooperation and Arts Council England, London.
Questo libro è stato tradotto grazie a un contributo alla traduzione assegnato dal Ministero degli Affari Esteri e della Cooperazione Internazionale italiano.

Supported using public funding by
ARTS COUNCIL ENGLAND

Published in the UK by Dedalus Limited
24-26, St Judith's Lane, Sawtry, Cambs, PE28 5XE
email: info@dedalusbooks.com
www.dedalusbooks.com

ISBN printed book 978 1 910213 97 1
ISBN ebook 978 1 912868 39 1

Dedalus is distributed in the USA & Canada by SCB Distributors
15608 South New Century Drive, Gardena, CA 90248
email: info@scbdistributors.com   web: www.scbdistributors.com

Dedalus is distributed in Australia by Peribo Pty Ltd
58, Beaumont Road, Mount Kuring-gai, N.S.W. 2080
email: info@peribo.com.au

First published in Italy in 2016
First published by Dedalus in 2021

Lagunario copyright © *Isabella Panfido 2016*
This translation has been made possible thanks to the mediation of R.Vivian Literary Agency Padova, Italy

Translation copyright © Christine Donougher 2021

The right of Isabella Panfido to be identified as the author and Christine Donougher as the translator of this work has been asserted by them in accordance with the Copyright, Designs and Patents Act, 1988.

Printed and bound in the UK by Clays Ltd, Elcograf S.p.A
Typeset by Marie Lane

This book is sold subject to the condition that it shall not, by way of trade or otherwise, be lent, resold, hired out or otherwise circulated without the publisher's prior consent in any form of binding or cover other than that in which it is published and without a similar condition including this condition being imposed on the subsequent purchaser.

City Noir
General Editor: Timothy Lane

VENICE NOIR:
THE DARK HISTORY OF THE LAGOONS

THE AUTHOR

Isabella Panfido lives and works in Venice and the Veneto. She has a degree in Russian Literature and Language and is an arts correspondent for the *Corriere del Veneto*. She is also a poet (her poetry has been translated into English, Spanish, Slovenian and Croatian), translator (from English and Russian) and literary critic for various publications.

THE TRANSLATOR

Christine Donougher was born in England in 1954. She read English at Cambridge University and after a career in publishing is now a freelance translator of French and Italian. Her translation of *The Book of Nights* by Sylvie Germain won the 1992 Scott Moncrieff Translation Prize and she has been shortlisted twice for The Oxford-Weidenfeld Translation Prize for *Night of Amber* in 1996 and for *Magnus* in 2009, both also by Sylvie Germain.

Her translations for Dedalus from Italian are *Senso (and other stories)* by Camillo Boito, *Sparrow (and other stories)* by Giovanni Verga, *Cleopatra goes to Prison* by Claudia Durastanti and *The Price of Dreams* by Margherita Giacobino.

PREMISE

*Venetorum urbs divina disponente
providentia in aquis fundata, aquarum
ambitu circumsepta, aquis pro muro
munitur: quisque igitur quoquo modo
detrimentum publicis aquis inferre
ausus fuerit, et hostis patrie
iudicetur: nec minore plectatur paena
quam qui sanctos muros patriae violasset.
Huius edicti ius ratum perpetuumque
esto.*

*The city of the Veneti by the will of divine
providence founded in water,
surrounded by water,
is protected by water instead of walls:
and therefore let whosoever in whatsoever manner
would dare to cause harm to the public waters
be judged an enemy of the city
and let him be punished with no less a penalty
than if he had violated the sacred walls of a city:
may the authority of this ruling be perpetually binding.*

Words penned by the humanist Giovambattista Cipelli, known as Egnazio (Venice 1473-1553), and engraved in gold on a black marble plaque erected at the seat of the Magistrature for the Waters at Rialto, now in the Correr Museum.

When the Lion roared there was no alternative but to submit, trembling, to its law.

This edict leaves no room for doubt, the waters of the Lagoon were – and are (or should be) – sacred, inviolable as the precincts of a temple, the boundaries of the city. The most fascinating part of this dictat – expressed in such categorical and exemplary terms as even now to strike a chord in the heart of every Venetian, if any such still exists – lies in the incisive introductory description of the Urbs Venetorum: founded, perforce, by divine will, the conurbation of the Veneti rose from the water, sank its own foundations into the waters and was surrounded and embraced by the waters. As though in an amniotic fluid, contained within an invisible membrane of *mestizza*, water that is neither sea nor river, neither salt nor fresh, hybrid water, resulting from the constant interaction of sea tides and river flow, water that is progeny of Father Ocean and Mother Earth, the water of the Lagoon.

But what in actual fact was the Lagoon?

A brackish basin of some 550 square kilometres, extending south-west to north-east, enclosed and separated from the sea by a thin cordon of sandbars punctuated by three Lagoon inlets: the ports of San Nicolò, Malamocco and Chioggia; divided, in relation to Venice, into the northern Lagoon and the southern Lagoon.

This is what we can see today when the aeroplane in which we are hypothetically flying circles over that variegated patch of water, speckled with little morsels of land, singed with graduated shades of blue green.

But what today lies beneath our shining eyes, which just cannot get used to the sight of this miniaturised marvel and its patent heart-rending fragility, has not always been like this.

Without presuming to speak for the geographer or the historian, we will simply note that the Lagoon is a landscape in every sense of the word, that is to say the result of human intervention in a natural environment, which is inherently unstable. We know it is about six thousand years old – this the experts have established with some degree of certainty, thanks to a "birth certificate", consisting of a core sample obtained in 1971 by drilling into the floor of the Lagoon to a depth of 950 metres in the area of the island of Tronchetto: it showed a first layer of about 9 metres of foraminiferal deposits – that is, protozoa with shells – of Lagoon origin, dating to the Holocene epoch, but beneath this, and extending 63 metres into the core, the sediment is of continental origin dating back to the Pleistocene; so the identity card of our beloved, brackish Eden-in-miniature tells us that the Lagoon is very young compared with the age-old Earth.

And traces of artefacts attest to a human presence from

the second millenium BC; we know that the Romans were well acquainted with some of the Lagoon's attractions but it is only from the sixth century AD that permanent settlements were established. Places grew up of legendary fame, sites of resistance to the barbarian invasions but also small centres of civilisation that left extremely fertile seeds: Altino, Spina, Costanziaca, Ammiana, populated by peoples who came from the hinterland to the north and south of the Lagoon basin.

The strange thing – as related to us by the writer Jacomo Filiasi (who knew a great deal and what he did not know he imagined) – is that a sort of Lagoon aristocracy soon became established, a kind of division between indigenes and outsiders, based on areas of provenance and settlement: so in the old chronicles the Patavini, Atestini, Montesilicani and Vicentini, who had settled in the central and lower Lagoon, were considered non-Venetian, whereas on the other hand the Aquilejesi, Concordiesi, Opitergini, Altinati, Feltrini and Acelani could claim to be of Venetian origin. It is difficult to get into the mindset of that time, but after all there is nothing new under the sun if even today the residents of Upper Castello, true heirs of the founders of the City distance themselves from the residents of Lower Castello, a motley crew of Greeks, Armenians, Dalmatians and more generally Levantines who only arrived in the City six or seven centuries ago, not to mention the feud – now laid to rest not by reconciliation but by depopulation – between the Arsenalotti and the Barnabotti.

But let us leave to its inauspicious fate the City that every day sees the countdown of its residents recorded in the implacable flashing-red digital figures in the little window of the pharmacy in Campo San Bartolomeo, alias San Bartolo, at the feet of a snickering Carlo Goldoni, one who was far-sighted with regard to the degeneracy of his fellow citizens. Triggering furious anger alternating with resigned discouragement, the bitter observation, every day and at every step, of the irredeemable vulgarity that has now destroyed this blessed plot, fallen from heaven or risen from the abyss, prevents me from finding any way to speak of the ineffable magic I still recognise, at night when it is inhabited only by rats and by its few citizens – rather less numerous and bold than the rats – or in the thick November fog when the more crass and tacky local commerce is temporarily hidden from view, allowing the seeping, fading stucco renderings to emerge, the only true heirs of the glorious age of Venetian colourism.

Too many pages, words, images have been heaped on the Unnamed wonder for me to dare add any more: every syllable about the City, in the writing or the reading, would sound trivial, banal, inadequate. And Calvino's Marco Polo has taught us the only way to speak of it is to do so indirectly.

So I will not say another word about the agony and the ecstasy of the Unnamed, that miracle of equilibrium built on a few millimetres of grey silty clay, the "caranto", a providential stratum, resulting from the leaching through rainwater of surface carbonates during the Holocene epoch. Were it not for the caranto, my Thaïs of white stone, you would never have existed.

But if we circumnavigate the tortured wonder with indirect words, like concentric circles round the point of origin, talking of something else, we will nevertheless remain within its echo range, caught in the snare of the place's magic, of its violent and glorious history, of its proud and shrewd people, at the heights of yesteryear and in the depths of the present day.

We will keep away from the dense nucleus of ineffable beauty and instead roam the sacred walls that are its waters, with a strange chart that does not follow any predetermined routes but those of caprice and imagination, getting about in a little boat suited to the shallow floor of the Lagoon, along canals and *ghebi* (creeks), skirting *barene* (saltmarshes) and *velme* (mudflats), without a nautical map, without a marine licence, aquatic flâneurs, abandoning ourselves to the calming atmosphere of the Lagoon; to its seductive and innocent mutability (closed in by long fingers of sand and yet ever open, with its mouths receptive to the wooing of the Adriatic) to being what is, land and water in constant evolution; to its elusiveness, like that of a scent that lingers and disappears, like music that fades away without visible trace.

So how can one describe the volatile essence of an organism in perpetual mutation, of a shimmering reflection on a liquid surface in continuous minimal motion, of a body of water and light? By starting with the solid reality of facts.

The starkness of the figures is much more dramatic and explicit than any comment: in the last three centuries the *barene* have been reduced from 160 to 47 square kilometres; in the years from 1979 to 1990 the Lagoon lost 25 million cubic metres of its solid mass, washed out to the open sea – this has also led to its invasion by a million more cubic metres of water per year, thereby causing an increasing flattening of the Lagoon floor, with the silting-up of the deep canals and the erosion of the shallows, with the obvious transformation of animal and vegetable habitats. And we prefer not to think of what will happen – but is already happening – with the new steel palisade of biblical nomenclature.[1]

But the fascination of this ever-changing environment, of this little womb of earth and water that has given birth to the great City that was the Serenissima, is so commanding, so resurgent at every outing on the Lagoon, and the continually disavowed but never eradicated pride of belonging to this place is so strong, that I will try to describe it, by telling little stories, some based on events, historical facts or personal memories, some entirely invented, since, as we know, the truth of the imagination is the most comforting of possible truths.

---

[1] Translator's note: A reference to the controversial MOSE scheme (the acronym derives from the name of a prototype floodgate, the (Modulo Sperimentale Elettromeccanico), consisting of 78 mobile gates intended to block the flow of sea water into the lagoon in the event of exceptionally high tides. Critics include those who fear a negative environmental impact as well as those opposed to its design and to its funding, which has given rise to legal accusations and prosecutions for fraud and corruption. Mose is the Italian spelling of the Biblical prophet Moses.

FATA MORGANA

Today I am breaking a promise.

And the person who bound me to silence when he confided to me the mysterious event will, from the seamen's empyrean where he now dwells, forgive me; but the chance encounter in the library with some memorable pages by nobleman Jacomo Filiasi has convinced me that what happened to Captain Amedeo Piazza was not the fruit of a colourful imagination or of a celestial vision but a very rare yet recurrent phenomenon in the Lagoon.

So, drawing on an oral account heard by a little girl – some decades ago, therefore – I will now try to relate as accurately as I can the extraordinary occurrence witnessed by Captain Piazza.

VENICE NOIR

One afternoon in late November some forty years ago, the famed, unforgettable tugboat captain Amedeo Piazza, in the small wheelhouse of the *Strenuus*, moored on the Riva dei Sette Martiri, with the basin of San Marco before it immersed in a milky obscurity that muffled every sound and blanketed everything within sight, related to a little girl bundled up in a loden coat, the amazing thing that, as I have discovered today, the nobleman Filiasi, too, stumbled upon one hundred and fifty years earlier, more or less in the same place.

You need to know that Captain Piazza, a little under two metres tall, with a gaunt face divided in half by a blond drooping moustache above a mouth almost as thin as a scratch line, was widowed at a very young age, when his wife died delivering a stillborn, first child. A tragedy for which Amedeo Piazza had only partly consoled himself, blotting out his personal life in manic and grief-crazed work as a seaman. His was an illustrious and unblemished career: already a master mariner by the age of twenty-three, right from the outset, first as second pilot, very soon afterwards as captain, he had always worked on Venetian tugboats, even during the Second World War when the tugboat service in the port was used solely by the naval fleet, all the vessels still in operation after sinkings and various other losses in the dangerous waters of the Mediterranean having been requisitioned.

At the time this story was told in that floating little tower of sturdy sheet metal, suspended eight metres above the surface of the water and surrounded by fog, Captain Piazza must have been about fifty years old, but that is a calculation I make today, certainly not based on the impression of a child to whom of course that austere and imposing man with the gentlest blue eyes appeared an old man.

Given his age, on the verge of retirement, those in charge of the work rosters tried to spare him the night shifts and long trips in the southern Mediterranean, assigning him however the more difficult jobs, those rescue operations on the high seas, especially with the *bora* wind raging, and fortunately very rare, which only he could tackle and accomplish without loss of life or vessel.

When it came to rescuing men and watercraft in impossible conditions, no one was better acquainted than he with the treacherousness of the Adriatic and its shallows, no one had better mastery than he of the heroic resources of those funny squat boats with the rounded bows and orange funnels. His mere presence drew attention, his slightly gravelly voice, always low-pitched, more from instinctive reserve than a natural tonality, cut through any background noise, whether human or mechanical.

No one knew better than Captain Piazza how, in a few words – brevity being a quality of leadership – to get to the nub of the matter and to the hearts of his crew. The seamen under his command perhaps feared him a little but they obeyed, first out of duty, then out of respect and absolute trust.

In that late afternoon the little girl in the loden coat had been taken to visit the *Strenuus*, which had only just arrived from the shipyard in Chioggia, a brand-new technological gem and flagship of the fleet moored at Riva dei Sette Martiri, right in front of the Cornoldi Barracks, formerly known as Palazzo Molin delle Due Torri, where, according to a stone inscription,

Francesco Petrarch lived for seven years as a guest of the government of La Serenissima.

Captain Piazza, who always showed an understandable, touching attentiveness towards children, had taken charge of the little girl and brought her into his wheelhouse, holding in his own long bony hand – that of a violinist rather than a seaman – the little red-gloved hand at the end of a recently fractured and badly mended right arm. The over-sized loden trailed on the metal rungs of the steep ladder leading from the deck to the wheelhouse, but the captain's firm and secure grip brought the coat safely up the steps to the door of the wheelhouse. In the quiet hum of that wheelhouse, illuminated by little red and green control lights, Amedeo Piazza sat the child on the pilot's tall wooden stool and, with narrowed blue eyes staring out at the blanket of fog on the other side of the turret window, began to describe the invisible geography of an evanescent and silent Lagoon.

The child followed Captain Piazza's long figure as it drew on the glass a secret map of islands. On every detail of this phantom map the index finger rested for a moment, the time it took for a voice roughened by long nights of salt wind to disclose in a whisper the names of those invisible places: San Servolo, San Lazzaro degli Armeni, San Clemente, and then up in a straight line, out to the right Santo Spirito, Poveglia… then the finger with a nail like a perfect almond, moved to the left: La Certosa, Le Vignole – the child liked the fruity sound of this name – Sant'Erasmo.

After a pause Captain Piazza, turning his face a few degrees, said, "San Michele." The little girl in the loden coat wriggled a bit and for the first time, opening a breach in the wall of her timidity, chipped in, saying, "I know that place, that's where papa is, mamma takes me there every Sunday morning."

Amedeo Piazza, standing with his back against the big pale wooden wheel of the helm in the restricted space of the wheelhouse, reaches out his hand and lightly touches her head with the hint of a caress: "I know, I knew your papa well. Every now and then I go and pay a visit to him as well. That's where my little boy is, on San Michele."

A long pause follows, fortunately interrupted by an indecipherable crackling of electrical discharge emanating from the tugboat's radio. And at that very moment Captain Piazza decides to tell her a secret.

This is the way he begins: "Now I'm going to tell you a story I've never told anyone else. It's a real secret, but I trust you and I am sure you won't tell a soul."

Wrapped in her loden coat the little girl starts to shiver.

No one had ever told her a secret before, no one had ever treated her with such seriousness, it meant assuming enormous responsibility, keeping the words all to herself for ever, held in the wide-meshed net of memory.

But as we know, a small child's memory is an inviolable safe, all the events of a whole lifetime leave some childhood memories absolutely intact, perfect in their fullness of detail and in their verbal accuracy. All the more so in the case of a secret.

Captain Piazza's face in the shadows of the wheelhouse had become solemn and, if possible, even longer and thinner.

"The Lagoon is a strange place," he began, opening wide his arms inside the sleeves of a jacket of dark blue cloth that he wore on board – it was double-breasted and had gold buttons that gleamed in the dimness of the wheelhouse, "it's like a huge labyrinth of water with long thin strips of sand akin to snakes curled up in the shallows. There are areas you can only get to in small flat-bottomed rowing boats because any normal vessel would run aground, some channels allowing a draught of only twenty, thirty centimetres.

"And being as I am, unable to remain on dry land when I am not on a tug, I get into my little *s'ciopon* – you know, one of those small boats that were used for duck shooting – and I go out into this beautiful labyrinth of water, taking a fishing rod with me, and a net, for you never know, I might catch something for my supper, then I'll cook it at home in the evening."

He uses a great many expansive, controlled gestures to season his words with the greatest possible detail: for "fishing" he raises the palm of his hand vertically, spreading his thumb and little finger as wide apart as possible; for "flat-bottomed" he leans forward from the waist drawing in the long neck that emerges from his shirt collar; for "labyrinth" he wiggles all ten fingers at the same time, as if playing a piano.

The child is totally captivated, just like one of those fish that Captain Piazza would hook from his *s'ciopon*.

"I go wherever the boat takes me, I try to go with the flow, in other words with the movement of the incoming and outgoing tides in the Lagoon, so sometimes I find myself where I would not have expected to be. But the beauty of it is exactly that: to lose track a little, to forget everything else and just look at what is around you."

A little voice asks, "But aren't you afraid of not finding the way home?"

What a naive question to put to someone like Captain Piazza. The answer comes in the form of a smile, followed by the words, "No, there's no danger of really losing your way in the Lagoon, all you have to do is take your bearings from the bell towers on the islands, you know, the way people used to in the countryside. The Lagoon is basically like the countryside only instead of land there's water, big fields of water. So you just have to look for a belltower, there are lots all around us, and you soon get your bearings: of course you need to be a little familiar with this waterland, but I know my way around pretty well. However, what I wanted to tell you happened not far from that island we both know well: San Michele.

"I had gone to take a rose to my son and to his mother, who keep each other company beneath a little white cross. When I came out of the cemetery, I got back into my *s'ciopon*, which I had left moored on the waterfront, and going with the current, I headed the boat in the direction of San Francesco del Deserto. I rowed, trying to keep out of the main channels because of the waves, but there was no disturbance, there was no one to be seen out in that heat. The air was still, as still as the water, which looked like glass.

"It must have been six in the evening because the cemetery had closed its gates right behind me; but in summer – it was the end of June – the sun was still beating down.

"That stretch of Lagoon is wild, the odd *barena*" – he breaks off to see if there is a questioning look in the child's eyes, then carries on – "the odd strip of sand with tufts of grass on it and only far, far away towards south can you make out a darker line, which is the island of Sant'Erasmo. However, on that particular late afternoon there was nothing visible on the horizon, perhaps because of the heat creating a veil of haze, and not a sound, just like it is now. I was rowing and listening to the drip from the oars and the little splash when they went into the water alternating with the backwash when they came out – that was the only sound around me. A good rhythm that accompanied my thoughts. They were not dark thoughts, just a bit sad: I wondered why my little boy should never have been able to learn from his father to do something as wonderful as go out on the Lagoon in a boat. And I pictured the imaginary scene of him standing, as big as you are now, with me behind him in the stern, pushing on the crossed oars, with my hands on top of his to guide his movements.

"In short, I was sad and also angry with life, with God, with the world. And I rowed more energetically to give vent to my feelings, heading for San Francesco del Deserto, where I would stay overnight with the monks, as I sometimes did. It is a place that does the heart good, that island, with its tranquillity, the peacocks under the cypress trees, in the midst of the deep silence of the Lagoon; it was just the right place to bring a bit of serenity to my thoughts.

"Suddenly, some one hundred metres from the prow, looking northwards, the water undergoes a transformation and I see in front of me a wide band of the most dazzling intense pink. Above it, just above it, where a moment before there was nothing, there appears, as if someone had rested it upon the surface of the water, a large green island, densely covered with treetops and lower down bushes of yellow and blue and pink.

You understand? An island suspended above that blade of pink light. There, where a moment before was nothing.

"I freeze, my oars in mid-air, and stop breathing as well. I cannot believe my eyes. But wait, that's not all: the water further away, on either side of the pink band, rises, but not like a wave, no, there was no movement, everything was still; the water – but it is difficult even just to imagine it – simply swelled, as if it were rising, on a steady incline, think of a hill. That's it, the water becomes convex, rounded, silvery, it rises skywards, like an enormous iridescent bubble. And above that silver the sky is drained of blue and becomes pure transparent light, like a diamond."

Amedeo Piazza breaks off, looking for something in the surrounding fog, some word, some meaning, some explanation to offer those two rounded eyes in the gloom; then he resumes, focusing on a distant point, visible only to him: "I knew there was nothing there, it was impossible for an island to have come into being within a second, I knew the Lagoon was flat and that water cannot climb upwards. I knew, I knew all that, yet what I saw was as real as the image of you here in front of me. I stayed motionless, standing in the stern, clutching my two crossed oars for I do not know how long. I have thought about it many times since then, I have tried to work out for how many minutes that marvel remained visible for me alone. I confess I wept with emotion: I thought it was a sign my son was sending me to communicate what he had not been able to tell me, to demonstrate his presence, to console me. It was simply and truly beautiful, a gift that someone had actually wanted me to have. I don't know, I don't know what happened or why; I certainly saw that extraordinary thing with these very eyes and the whole thing was bright and magical and deeply moving.

"Then it was gone, suddenly, just as it had appeared, without a sound, without any movement.

"The surrounding water became flat once more, the horizon clear, the blue sky already darkened in the east. In the absolute silence there was not even the cry of a seagull nor a breath of wind. Flat calm, the air was clear and serene, as I was myself, because that thing, that island in the light had given me immense happiness."

The ever deeper voice of Amedeo Piazza died away with a little sigh, a faint exhalation. The little girl's hands held tight Captain Piazza's hand and her memory held tight his words.

And if today that pact of secrecy has been broken and that unforgettable account by Captain Piazza has taken a written form, the reason lies in the lines printed below, taken from chapter XX, entitled "Fata Morgana", from the book *Memorie storiche de' veneti primi e secondi* by the scholar Jacomo Filiasi, which, as you will see, explain the magnificent mystery.

"*...In the lagoon between Torcello and Venice there is sometimes to be seen an optical illusion that as far as we know no one has ever commented upon. It appears more frequently in the northern part of our lagoon. (...) Various images are to be seen, produced by the reflected and refracted light, and even more so by the modifications to which the light is subject by the gases in the air and by whatever molecules are released at certain times, or undergo some sort of alteration in the water* *and the air, etc. In that part of the lagoon that lies within the sandbars of Sant'Erasmo, Treporti, Venezia and Murano, the Fata Morgana customarily appears.*

Rarely, however, does it manifest itself, and in fact we ourselves have seen it only twice in many years. Between the above-mentioned sandbars and Murano (and the islets of San Michele and San Cristoforo that lie between Murano and Venice) in the hottest and calmest days of summer, about three hours before sunset, the surface of the water appears as if raised and made convex.

On the surface of the water, looking towards the sandbars, there is to be seen what appears to be a broad area of milky brightness, and lying behind this a second band coloured blue, and then a third that is very white on which painted in even brighter colours are the verdant trees, hedges and houses that exist on the sandbars. So bright are those colours you might say the green of the plants was turned to emerald, and the white of the houses to silver. And the radiance of such images combined with the luminous mirror in which they are reflected and the vibrant blue band behind, together with the splendour of the third band yet further behind, beneath the sandbars, forms such a magical scene, it is impossible adequately to describe it. And in addition the convex shape, which these zones seem to take on in such a case, whereby the lagoon appears to rise and swell. (...) And in addition other areas that came into view afterwards, some almost crimson, others green, white, or blue. And in addition the sky behind the sandbars above the sea appeared so brilliantly clear, as if it were of crystal, the eye was almost blinded by its refulgence (...)".

ISLANDS

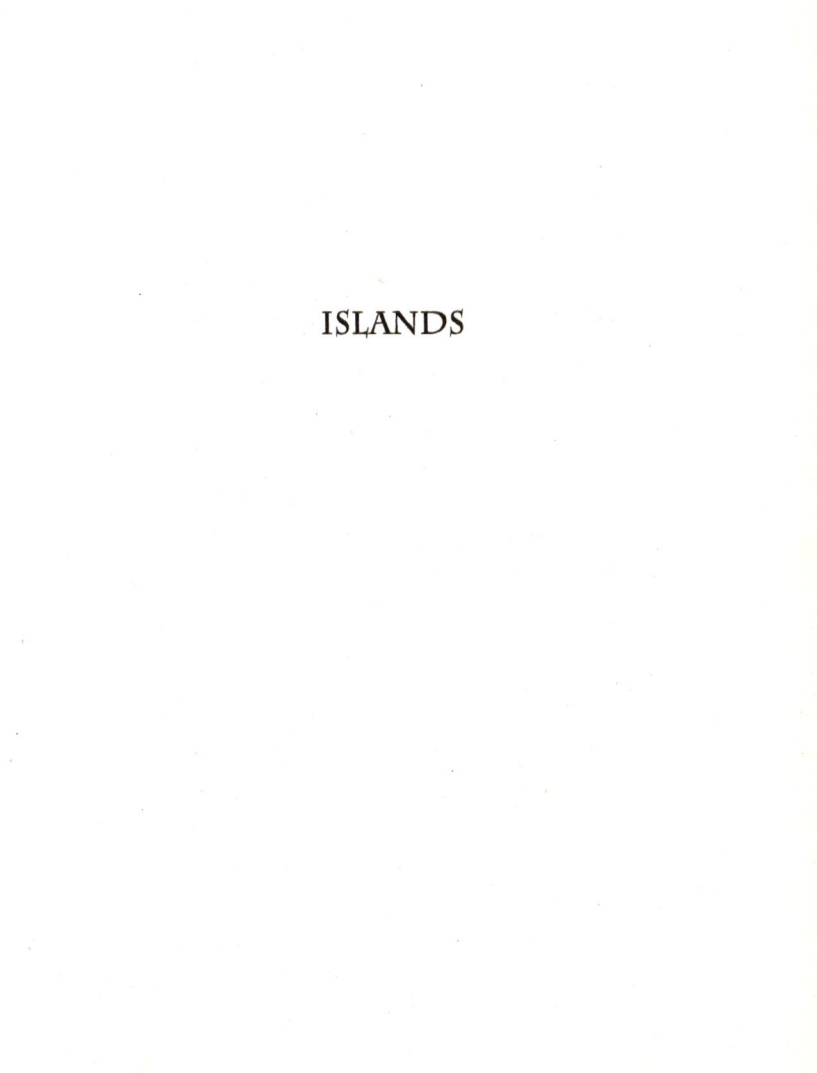

FISOLO

If you search the map of the Lagoon for the island of Fisolo you need good eyesight and patience. It is a tiny speck of sand and stone, completely abandoned to the dominion of brambles and locust trees, which as we know need very little to survive and with the determination of so-called "invasive" plants colonise every patch of land neglected by man.

Fisolo, which also gives its name to the canal leading to it that runs past Alberoni, has no illustrious history as the seat of a convent or of some ancient settlement: there is nothing to it.

The only reference you will come across to this speck of land will tell you that together with the nearby tiny islands of Podo and Campana it was used under the unhappy rule of the Austro-Hungarian Empire as a fort for the defence of the City against possible attacks, whether from the sea, via the historic southern entrance to the Lagoon, or from the mainland, Fisolo being relatively near the coast, now scarred by the industrial effluent from Marghera.

But there was a time when little Fisolo was, through no fault of its own, witness to a very sad story of which there is no trace to be found in the glorious chronicles of La Serenissima but which could well have been passed down – with compassionate discretion, without scandal or outrage – by the City's rumour mill, wagging tongues on the street, always hostile to the powerful and affectionate towards losers.

In Casa Renier, in Ramo San Zulian, nobleman Almorò, head of a large family of limited means, had taken the irrevocable decision whereby the fate of Chiara, the second and most beautiful of his five daughters, was to become a nun, and he had selected for her the convent of San Lorenzo which at that time, at the beginning of the sixteenth century, represented the best solution for settling without great expense the uncertain future of a young woman of illustrious lineage.

As happened all too often, the person directly concerned had no say with regard to her own fate and, obliged to obey the will of her parents, putting on a brave face, she resigned herself to the inevitable.

This submissiveness, however, was out of character in the determined and combative Renier girl who beneath an outward appearance of one of those Vivarini madonnas painted on a gold background, all radiant blonde hair and transparent rosiness, harboured the restless dreams and desires expressed in her eyes – eyes as grey as the waters of the Lagoon when the dark *bora* (north-easterly wind) blows.

Unlike her sisters, Chiara gave no thought to love, marriage, social life, clothes, chit-chat; none of the things normally belonging to the so-called feminine world were of any concern to her. She was prepared to dress like a young woman, yes; resigned to the conventions of being female, she wore with little enthusiasm, but with grace and ease, all the requisite paraphernalia for a sixteen-year-old girl of her penniless rank.

But her spirit was always elsewhere, far from the *portego* (central reception room) of the palazzo looking out over the Canale San Zulian; her thoughts rested beyond the waters she gazed at so intently from the quayside of the Piazzetta every morning after mass in San Marco.

The silhouettes of the ships moored there, with their dark mass against the early morning light, punctuated the busy expanse of the basin spread before Chiara's eyes like the most exciting theatre in the City.

The strong smell that filled the air on the waterfront carried intimations of a new world, as unfamiliar as it was yearned for: the spices, pepper above all, at once subtle and aggressive, the tar on the hulls, the hemp of the ropes, the salt-impregnated jute of the sacks of merchandise, the waxed canvas of the furled and inert sails, vinegar emptied on to the ground from barrels waiting to be washed out and readied for refilling with new wine to be taken aboard, the dominant smell of mustiness from the open hatches of the empty holds. But above all the sweat of bodies, which imbued every board of decking, every plank of the vessel, every oar, every batten in the hold: that essence of man, that sublimate of exertion, adventure and life.

This was the smell of the world she dreamed of, this the air that pervaded her desires.

To board ship, set sail, and slowly, mile by mile, explore the coastlines she had memorised, all the ports and docks on the eastward route, along the Istrian and Dalmatian littoral, and then, further down, to the Morea and into the open waters round the Aegean islands. Every evening in her father's *mezza* (mezzanine office) she studied in secret the nautical charts and portolan maps that Almorò kept in the black cupboard along with the charter agreements for his old ramshackle fleet of three *rascone* (large twin-ruddered river cargo boats) and two *bragozzi* (Adriatic fishing boats). That web of black lines fanning out from the small basin of San Marco that Chiara knew by heart, that her eyes had sketched out every day of her life ever since she could remember, those arabesques of tiny letters penned in red ink, the names of all the ports of call on the Adriatic sea, were open-petalled flowers that bloomed on the meandering coastline that descended headlong towards a universe of lands and waters redolent of the air from which she drew nourishment every morning as from her daily bread, her mental oxygen.

Chiara well knew that no one would have understood her world and she had confided to no one the confused longings that filled her young heart.

How could her father have possibly understood?

She had tried every avenue of persuasion to convince him: she knew that being his favourite she had a strong influence over him; she had cajoled him with her voice accompanied by the harpsichord, singing and playing for him alone in the evening before going to sleep; she had wept, giving reasons – she wanted to live in the world and not die of boredom within the walls of a convent – bathing Almorò's pale hands with genuine tears; she had shouted with rage, tearing the lace from her bodice, pleading to stay at home, to study the music she so loved, to serve as housekeeper and thereby earn her keep and if she was not to be spared from becoming a nun, at least let them send her to the Pietà, to join the novices' choir. From the convent on the waterfront she would at least have watched the ships entering and leaving the basin every day, she would have been able to breathe in the smell of distant lands carried in their half-spread sails during their slow progression into the San Marco basin.

This "sea-sickness" that caused young Chiara to suffer and tremble was rooted in the past.

Almorò Renier, like many of the noble citizens of the bustling and wealthy Venice of the sixteenth century, had been a prosperous and enterprising ship owner: his fortune was made on the opposite Adriatic coast.

Before they had even turned twenty he and his elder brother Marco had moved to Istria to supervise at close hand a flourishing trade in wood and stone from Dalmatia, which their father had set up, in addition to the already lucrative activity of importing cloth from Flanders. Over some ten years the two young Reniers had managed to build up a fine fleet of ten sturdy *rascone* and eight *bragozzi* that crossed the shallow but by no means safe waters of the Gulf of Venice, leaving the port of Rovigno twice a week laden with cargo.

Of the two brothers it was Marco, two years the elder,

who was skilful at negotiating the purchase of the great treetrunks from the inland forests that arrived on the docks with the resin still seeping from them; he always managed to settle on a price lower than that for the previous consignment, finding fault with the goods for some different reason every time – the trunks were too thin, or too crooked, or too knotted – to obtain considerable reductions on the market price. And it was the same with the large blocks of white stone that arrived on enormous barges from the Dalmatian island of Brac. Marco was a born trader, worthy scion of the Renier dynasty; Almorò, more reserved, by natural inclination devoted to music and literature, went along with his brother's decisions, at heart grateful to be charged with secondary tasks – keeping the accounts and recording the departures and arrivals of the cargoes sent by sea.

Their affairs prospered. They built a white palazzo by the docks where the ships were loaded, with two double-arched windows on the piano nobile looking out over the waterfront and with small square windows on the mezzanine floor. There, on the *mezza*, were two solid writing desks made of walnut and a studded iron safe in which were kept the contracts for the purchase of goods and a few purses stuffed with silver coins. From the windows of the *mezza* they could keep a controlling eye on the departure of the ships, laden with goods right up to the loadline, and the arrival of those returning from Venice, less weighed down but carrying small wonders – fabrics, food, inlaid furniture, mirrors – that made easier the life of the Renier brothers and their compatriots, generous buyers of these objects, testimony to the elegance of their former Venetian existence. It pained them to be away from the great

City whose wealth and brilliance were like that of no other city in the world, Almorò even more than Marco, but the brothers knew that if they remained in Istria for another few years they would return to Venice rich and powerful, prepared for a life worthy of their family tradition.

Marco found complete satisfaction in trade, which totally absorbed him, he did not yet want to start a family, preferring to remain faithful to matrimonial ambitions that would afford him a prominent position in La Serenissima's political establishment. Meanwhile he concentrated on business, cultivating from a distance the network of contacts with those who mattered in the complex and delicate workings of the *Pregadi* (Senate), the real political heart of the Republic.

Almorò, on the other hand, of more modest aspirations, forbearing and reserved in character, had married young, sending for his betrothed to join him in Rovigno; of noble origin but very little fortune, Gaspara Zen was chosen by his father from the small number of young Venetian women prepared to go and live overseas.

Everything seemed to be going smoothly.

The trade to and from Venice increased year by year, the family grew – there were two boys Alvise and Tomaso, and two girls, Anna and Chiara – the palazzetto in the port began to look like a real Venetian palazzo, with fireplaces in every room and with its fine *portego* lined with green damask, where a harpsichord occupying a central position provided endless solace to the master of the house, who when at home would spend every moment of repose immersed in music.

But suddenly, in the space of a little more than a year, Almorò and the Renier's fine fleet were overwhelmed by misfortune.

His brother Marco, having sailed with a particularly valuable cargo he wanted to take care of personally, fell sick with a cerebral fever during the return voyage from the City and died within a week, at the end of a winter of raging north winds that only a month before had caused the loss of a convoy of eight of their largest ships, loaded to the gunnels, almost in view of the coast, off Parenzo, in the treacherously unpredictable waters of the Gulf of Venice.

To cap it all, the following summer poor Gaspara was unable to carry to term her fifth pregnancy and she died of an infection, leaving Almorò in despair, with four young children, deeply in debt for the goods lost in the shipwreck, incapable of taking fresh heart without his wife's affection and advice and his brother's boldness and business acumen. His melancholy nature got the better of him.

There was nothing for it but to return to La Serenissima, to his father's house, to seek help with the raising of those children and to try to start trading again with the little that was left to him.

So, having sold the palazzetto to a member of the Bon family who had recently moved to Istria for the salt trade, and kept the better furniture to take back with him – above all the harpsichord – with his children and furniture he set sail on the most solid *bragozzo*, the best of the surviving ramshackle fleet, and returned to the City, to his father's big dark house, which stood on the narrow Rio di San Zulian, where sunshine and fresh air were sporadic visitors.

There Almorò ended up by remarrying: "Thirty-five is too young to become a lifelong widower," old Renier had ruled, welcoming the family's new issue with the pragmatism of a

Venetian merchant. "Those four orphans need a mother."

Within a few months the *pater familias* found his son a new wife, concluding speedy matrimonial negotiations with an iron merchant from Brescia, a client of his with a twenty-year-old daughter to marry off, one who was "plain but healthy".

Incapable of going against his father and indifferent to his own fate, Almorò bowed to the patriarch's decisions, at heart grateful to the old *paron* (master) for taking charge of his life.

He settled in the rooms on the third floor, had another three children, getting by with some maritime trade, chartering and a little buying and selling from the house in which he was born and was never more to leave.

In that modestly comfortable house Chiara, who was two when her mother died, had grown up: the young stepmother, a good soul but sad and taciturn, with an ugly accent, of limited intelligence and irredeemably peasant origin, she showed no particular affection towards the children of her husband's first marriage, whom, guided by instinct rather than by calculation, she treated with cold respect, like special guests but complete outsiders.

Of her Istrian past, of the financial disaster, and of being born by the sea in a land fragrant with the smell of pines and myrtle, Chiara – like her siblings, moreover – knew nothing.

She had a vague and affectionate conception of her dead mother, who remained a presence in her life thanks to a miniature, a little portrait on wood, dating back to his "long-distance" engagement, that her father kept in a little casket on the bureau in the *mezza* and which Chiara took a peek at every day with mixed feelings of tenderness and pain.

Diffidently but with a vague and persistent sense of guilt,

Almorò had never wanted to reopen that painful chapter of Rovigno with his children, to tell them about that life, so very different from now, a life that was serene and bright like the palazzetto in the harbour, filled with reflections of the water and with sounds of the quayside; and out of respect for his silent nostalgia, no one close to him had ever spoken to the children of their Istrian past so as not to cause pain to Almorò, forever crushed by that lost happiness.

So, Chiara, sick with a nostalgia she could not explain to herself, unaccepting of her father's decision, saw herself doomed for life to a segregation she could not have endured. Far from the sea, from a view that extended beyond the near horizon of the San Marco quay, deprived of the unforgettable scent of nameless places that nevertheless spoke to her in a familiar language: no – she said to herself – she would not have survived even a month.

She tortured her imagination, trying to devise some means of deliverance from that cloistered fate, some way of escape.

Unexpectedly, as often happens, it was chance that offered her a possibility.

Every morning, when those few steps across the Piazzetta – from the entrance of the Basilica to beneath the two columns of Marco and Teodoro – along with the excitement of her anticipated encounter with the sea gave her a welcome sense of freedom from the bonds of her boring domestic life... every morning she caught the eye of a young commoner busy loading handcarts with merchandise from the ships moored on the waterfront.

Chiara paid attention only to the ships and the surrounding

water, to things that, as we have said, filled her imagination with sea voyages. However, that young lad, who was little more than a child, broke through her indifference towards her fellow human beings: she had first noticed a voice and only afterwards that small slight figure struggling along the jetties, stooped under inordinately large sackloads, with his face bowed but always smiling. That deep voice, incongruous for his age and stature, sang in some foreign language songs to a rapid heartbeat rhythm, deep but airy sounds.

"How strange," thought Chiara, "instead of huffing and puffing beneath his burden he even manages to find enough breath to sing."

One morning she responded with a smile to that voice and the voice changed, became even deeper and louder, while the lad passed so close by he brushed against her.

Chiara recognised the smell of the sea on him.

From that morning – it was the first of March, the beginning of the new year in the Venetian calendar – for days, as if by arrangement, their eyes would tell each other playful little things, always at arm's length and always wordless, only through looks and through his songs, which over time became so familiar to Chiara that they came back into her mind during the day, in the obscure, incomprehensible yet resonant form of that strangely familiar language she had never heard before.

Then, on the morning of the twentieth of March, with a light, warm, joyful *garbin* (south-westerly wind) blowing, Chiara spoke to him.

Without lowering her gaze, and in a vaguely anxious tone of voice, she asked him in what language were those songs of his.

"The language that's spoken across the sea," the lad replied, "in the forests. I was born in Cherso, a green and white island in the middle of a sea of such a blue as you have never seen here. My mother used to sing these songs to me when I was little, to send me to sleep, and I sing them now to send her my thoughts. It's been such a long time since she last saw me... but soon, finally, who knows, perhaps even tomorrow, I'll set sail for home."

This lad in his dark dusty jacket with the strong voice of a man had perfumed breath.

"Tomorrow? How will you get there? With which ship?"

Not with any ship, he was not old enough to embark as a sailor, they would not have taken him for another year, but – he explained – he was not going to wait another year, away from his beloved sea and white rocks and the pine woods as black as night even when the sun was high.

"I'm going in my boat," he added hurriedly, as if to reassure himself rather than Chiara: there was something of a pained pride that coloured his voice.

His father, who had brought him to Venice to work with him three years earlier, had died just over a month ago, killed by the effort of earning enough to buy himself a square-sailed boat and return to Cherso to work as a fisherman, independently and not for someone else as he had done all his life. And he had managed to buy it; of course the boat was not exactly new, money was tight, but they had fixed it up in a friend's boatyard at San Lorenzo, he and his father had caulked it, resealing the whole craft, and mended the sail, made a new tiller – in short, it was now sufficiently sound for the Gulf crossing, sound enough to take them home. His father had sworn they would put to sea in those early days of spring, to cross that northern basin of the Adriatic, which he knew to be devilish, and with the right wind finally return home.

He seemed to have learned this speech by heart, delivering it without pause, without drawing breath: he spoke Venetian well, but detectable in his pronunciation was a different, more sing-song inflection.

"The time has come," he added with the irrevocability of a long-considered decision. Tomorrow at dawn, with the wind in his favour, the *garbin* would speed him on his way from the greyness of the Lagoon to the deep blue waters of the Istrian coast.

That day Chiara too made her decision.

She secretly gathered together a few things: a small number of silver coins her father had set aside for her as a little nest egg in a small wooden box, a white smock and woollen jacket belonging to her elder brother, a little lambswool blanket she had had on her bed since she was born that was her comfort and refuge. With regard to shoes, she had to make do with the ones she wore in the house – her brother's sturdier leather shoes were much too big for her, making her stumble at every step and she would not have been able to move as quickly as she needed to. She spent that day gazing on things around the house and taking leave of them as if seeing them for the last time, finding that she felt both happy and sad, as happens on the eve of great turning-points in life.

She stayed awake all night: a hundred times she tiptoed from her bed to the window to check whether a favourable wind was still blowing, opening the window a fraction and leaning out just far enough to feel the breeze on her face. Then she would close the sashes and snuggle under the covers again, prey to an ever-increasing anxiety.

At very first light, in absolute silence so as not to wake her little sisters who slept in the same room, she got dressed in the clothes stolen from her brother, picked up her bundle of belongings, and holding her shoes in her hand crept down the dark staircase, knowing the number of steps by heart, cautiously opened the front door, unable to prevent a creak that sounded like thunder to her. Keeping her head down, she hurried as fast as she could the whole length of the silent and deserted Spadaria, turned right under the clock tower just as the bell of Sant' Alipio in the right-hand pinnacle of the Basilica began striking for matins. She was breathless by the time she had crossed the Piazzetta to the waterfront, where everyday working life was already starting up again: as yet only a few men aboard the ships were moving around sluggishly, throwing into the sea bucketfuls of dirty water, pulling in the slack mooring lines.

Despite her anxiety and understandable fear of being recognised by some servant or other – how stupid to have forgotten to wear a scarf over her head to disguise herself a little – she stood enraptured before the basin as it began to grow light: in the still-dense darkness above San Giorgio, from the thin line of the Lido came a silvery glimmer that was not yet light, like a low bright cloud that, reflected in the tranquil surface of the basin, expanded the area, doubling the distance between the Piazzetta quayside and the Punta della Dogana. And the waterfront of the Giudecca, in total darkness, looked to her like a long solid mass of brown seaweed floating in the gentle backwash that licked at the stone embankment beneath her frozen little feet. It was her first dawn, the dawn of the first day of spring, the dawn of the first day of real life: everything suddenly seemed to her natural, right, simple.

She thought she would write to her father as soon as she had made the sea-crossing, she would explain the reasons for her flight and he would understand and forgive her. Sooner or later she was bound to return and perhaps even agree to become a nun. But later, much later: first she must travel, become acquainted with the sea, breathe.

She looked around: there was no sign of the lad from Cherso.

How stupid she had been, she had not asked him where he kept his boat, where he would leave from and at what time, and he certainly could not have guessed what her intention was.

Suddenly all certainties evaporated in the exposure of this plan of hers for what it was, so naive, so rash. Yet the thought of calling the whole thing off, of returning home – everyone was still asleep and no one would have noticed her reckless departure – never even crossed her mind.

There she stood, dry-eyed, stock-still, in front of the tall prows, fringed with seaweed, that bobbed up and down, lazily and wisely like the heads of old bearded men, deep black on those dark waters. Meanwhile, to her right, the market slowly began to come to life: large baskets full of vegetables from Vignole and Sant'Erasmo were being unloaded from the first *sandoli* (Lagoon boats used for fishing and hunting).

The fresh smell of fennel – she was such a glutton for fennel – came to her nostrils like a caress, an injection of optimism.

Then, trying to reconstruct the few words the lad from Cherso had spoken, she recalled that he had mentioned the yard where the boat was kept: at San Lorenzo he had said. She then convinced herself that to reach the basin he would go via Rio dei Greci. She got there in a flash, running like the wind along Riva die Schiavoni, with her bundle under her arm. She felt as if her legs could no longer support her, she was trembling with cold, excitement and exhaustion.

The waterfront was empty and an icy wind swept across the *masegni* (Venice's paving stones of Euganean trachyte) that looked even greyer than usual in the wan light of daybreak.

Suddenly, from the left, from Rio dei Greci, there emerged into the basin a square sail with a big white star on it that no sooner felt the air in the basin than it instantly swelled, making a strange, and in that silence loud, sucking sound. Chiara heard the slightly husky voice singing a song in that unknown language.

Here he was.

Chiara had no name to call out – they had only exchanged a few words and certainly not their names – but she began to wave her arms, to jump up and down, shouting at the top of her lungs: "Oyee, Cherso, wait for me, I'm coming with you across the sea."

As soon they left the basin of San Marco the sail filled even better with the wind: the rudder was sturdy, the boat smelt of tar and the coiled hemp ropes in the bow in the first light of dawn on that twenty-first day of March resembled a flat round world served up to them to satisfy their hunger to be on their way.

They soon left behind the outline of San Clemente and

Santo Spirito, pointing the little prow south-westwards, to reach the open sea at San Pietro. The boy held the rudder and adjusted the sail effortlessly, confident of what he was doing, despite the wind that stiffened minute by minute. The boat had a shallow draught – the boy reassured himself – there was no risk of running aground on the shoals in the southern Lagoon network of *velme* and *ghebi*.

Yet something was wrong, the direction of the wind had changed.

It was not the light south-westerly *garbin* blowing that morning, the wind that would easily have carried them eastwards out to the open sea; it was an anomalous and untimely dark *bora* that had suddenly got up as night ended, which flattened the sail towards the westward side of the Lagoon.

The wind strengthened and the young sailor had not enough experience or muscle-power to handle those furious north-easterly gusts that buffeted the little craft as if it were made of paper. They began to take on water and the inadequacy of the *sessola* (wooden bailer) that Chiara frantically filled from the bottom of the boat and emptied over the side immediately became obvious. Soaked to the skin, their legs now totally immersed in water that completely covered the *pagioli* (wooden floor slats), they found no words to comfort each other, just terrified glances.

In search of shelter they entered the Canale di Fisolo, turning right and allowing the sail to swell and swell until the white star entirely filled the sky above them. The sail, stretched to the maximum, began to tear away at the sides and then, suddenly, in an extremely violent icy blast of wind, with a strange sound, like the roar of a wild animal, it split down the middle, blasting the white star, and the sky above, as black as night.

It was three days before a fisherman found them lying on the sand on little Fisolo, home to crabs and seagulls.

The broken boat had run aground a little further towards the islet of Podo, mastless, rudderless and oarless.

Chiara and the lad from Cherso appeared to be sleeping in tranquillity, their heads side by side, their faces turned to the east, their staring eyes continuing to gaze up at the sky, fixed on a point invisible to the living, a place of rest and joy, far away, across the sea.

SANT'ARIANO

Already at the end of the fifteenth century people spoke of Sant'Ariano under their breath.

There were many strange stories in circulation relating to that out-of-the-way island in the northernmost part of the Lagoon. Sant'Ariano himself, that is to say the martyr Adriano, was not in any way connected with the popular rumours spreading from island to island that eventually reached the Palazzo Ducale and the attentive ears of La Serenissima's Signoria and its three vigilant and powerful state inquisitors.

What kept recurring like a sad refrain in the denunciations posted into the Mouth of Truth, even the mere sight of which causes a certain unease today, was not the saint to whom the church on the island was dedicated but the animated days, and nights in particular, of the nuns who lived in supposed retreat on this small island in the Lagoon.

This island – which today looks in every respect like the inspirational model for Böcklin's famous and no less disturbing painting, Isle of the Dead – in the very distant past formed part of the larger island of Costanziaco at the mouth of the river Sile, before, long before, the river was redirected further eastwards by engineering works undertaken by the wise and far-sighted government of La Serenissima. Of the island city of Costanziaco, refuge of the Altinati, there remain two areas of land, the present-day islands of Sant'Ariano, referred to above, and La Cura; the rest, consisting of splendid monasteries and churches, has been absorbed into the sandbars' quiet geography, indifferent to the transience of things human.

But let us return to Sant'Ariano and its sorry fame.

Legend tells us that the great monastery that peopled the island with lively and refined young nuns, the flower of the Venetian aristocracy's young women, was the scene of a love story that if not unhappy was certainly unusual, to say the least, and whose protagonists were Anna Michiel and Nicolò Giustinian.

Towards the end of the twelfth century there were between Venice and Byzantium a number of unresolved issues relating to the Dalmatian coast, which was contested by both sides and in truth not very happy under Venetian rule. Naval battles, alternately won and lost, took their toll on the government of the Duchy of Venice, which struggled, as its galleys were sunk and its crews wiped out, for temporary dominion over this or that coastal city. These were hard times for the maritime state, settlements on the mainland allied themselves with Barbarossa; Istrian and Dalmatian cities did not readily accept dominion passed off as protection by the Lagoon City; the king of Hungary was casting his greedy eye on the coast to snatch safe ports from the Venetian fleet; and, making the Gulf even more treacherous, Narentani and Almissani piracy posed a threat to navigation.

The situation was in continual flux, as fluid as the waters in the Gulf of Venice, which had been legally ratified as such under the terms of the Pactum Lotharii of 840. The Duchy also extended its own horizons along the west coast, committing fleets and men to defend the Adriatic below Ravenna, below Ancona. The hugeness of the task was matched by the will to establish at least a commercial dominance of the Adriatic.

But let us not stray too far off the subject, we need to get back to Anna.

Her father, Doge Vitale II Michiel, having set sail with one hundred galleys armed to the crow's nest and headed for Constantinople with the intention of teaching the emperor a lesson, had not only suffered a terrible defeat against the Byzantine leader, losing so much of the fleet and so many of the brave Venetian aristocrats who had sailed with him to fight against the greedy Oriental power, but, obliged to make dishonourable landfall on the Aegean island of Chios, had also seen the survivors of the battle decimated by the plague.

Returning to the Lagoon, let us say with his tail between his legs, he had moreover brought the plague to the City. It is easy to imagine the reception he got from his fellow citizens, who, even more then than now, did not forgive failure: as he emerged from the Doge's traditional visit to the nuns in the convent of San Zaccaria, on the second day of Easter in the distant and fateful year of 1172, he was attacked by a hothead and killed on the spot. Indeed, he was buried in that very church of San Zaccaria, not the one we marvel at today, enlarged and embellished by Marco Coducci and wonderfully endowed with one of Giambellino's most beautiful altarpieces, but in its earlier more basic form, traces of which are visible today in the crypt and the Cappella d'Oro.

However, in the course of this whole unfortunate episode, Vitale had also brought about the demise of the once glorious Giustinian dynasty – all the family's male members having been killed in the decisive and calamitous battle against the Byzantines. Extinction guaranteed – but for one shy and gentle Giustinian, the youngest and mildest Nicolò, who had become a monk in the monastery of San Nicolò del Lido because he had no interest at all in worldly pomp and glory, entirely dedicated as he was to prayer and retreat: that Nicolò was recalled to earthly vanities by ancestral duty.

In other words, he was obliged temporarily to suspend his vows of chastity and prayer, and to practice instead that of obedience.

To satisfy the will of his family and the needs of the Duchy – our pearl of the Lagoon was not yet La Dominante or Serenissima – he was obliged to marry the daughter of the very man who had richly contributed to the near extinction of the noble name of Giustinian and caused his forced return to the world of the laity.

He married Anna, daughter of Vitale Michiel, who although a nun, provided history with a good number of male Giustinian offspring, thanks to the recovered reproductive energies of the former monk, Nicolò. After many pregnancies and many painful deliveries, and having made sure of a good number – seven, it is said – of male descendants of the Giustinian line, Anna entrusted her sons to the loving care of the ducal government, which, like a good father, instilled in the young aristocrats it raised both the maritime and the mercantile virtues, and she returned to her monastic devotions, as her spouse, the meek and productive Nicolò, also returned to his.

Probably in tribute – fully deserved tribute – to her virtuous motherhood, she was allowed to take up residence on a distant island that lay on the most northerly edge of the Lagoon, that strip of sand where a few traces of the ancient settlement of Costanziaca were still preserved.

There Anna, dedicated to prayer and committed to a life of religious devotion but conscious of the evils and deceptive pleasures of the world, founded a small refuge for young Venetian women who wanted to follow the divine calling, and she dedicated it to Sant'Ariano.

Mother Anna and her sisters spent their lives in prayer and in performing humble tasks in the serene light of that part of the Lagoon furthest from the sea, with the gentlest currents and the sweetest, least salty waters.

However, the uplifting epilogue to Anna's exemplary career did not save the island from the black book of La Serenissima's history, many, many years after the death of the fecund founder of the convent of Sant'Ariano.

During the golden age of La Serenissima, in fact, and with the corruption that power and wealth inevitably bring with them, the girls who voluntarily entered the cloister on

Sant'Ariano, answering the call of spiritual love, became ever fewer, while there was an increasing number of aristocratic young ladies compulsorily enrolled in the monastic life because of pragmatic family interests, the families being determined their patrimony should not be consumed in dowries for younger daughters.

So what happened at Sant'Ariano was what happened in so many other monasteries of the City: despite the prohibitions and rules of the cloister, and with the advantage of Sant'Ariano's isolation, far removed as it was from any route to the centre, those unwilling nuns, those (not always) beautiful and spirited Venetian young ladies, found the worldly distractions they sought.

It was rumoured that on some summer nights the lamps on the prows of the gondolas making their way to and from the *cavana* (boat shelter) of the convent on Sant'Ariano illuminated the stretch of water that separated the island from the nearby islet of La Cura as if it were broad daylight. It is well known that passion – and passion is not love – is ignited even in the hearts of those who are most observant of the rules, and if the object of desire is inaccessible, then that ardour becomes immeasurably intense; so it is not surprising that ardent young lovers should not be put off by a few hours' vigorous rowing for the sake of joining their paramours in the seclusion of Sant'Ariano.

But punishment for those sins of the flesh soon put an end to the illumination of warm nights in the far north of the Lagoon.

The mythological version of events might be expressed thus: the gods, angered by the lascivious behaviour of the young vestals, sent a messenger in the form of a stork that carried in its beak two black serpents. As it flew over the island the celestial wader dropped the reptiles as a sign intended to convey the gods' displeasure. The snakes rapidly multiplied until they infested the whole island, including the buildings, forcing the vestals to abandon it in haste.

The agnostic version, on the other hand – indisputably ungodly, yet more likely – might give this account of what happened: one of those lovers in the habit of paying nocturnal visits to the island, having discovered his beloved with another enterprising visitor, decided to take his own revenge.

This betrayed young man, whom we shall call Alvise – there were, and there are now, so many Venetian men with this name, there can be no fear of any indiscreet identification – Alvise, therefore, got hold of one of those pots made of rushes used by fishermen to catch eel – round, with a hole in the top and a wooden lid. With the pot, he went to San Giuliano on the mainland, where, in the sand dunes behind the margins of the Lagoon, among tamarisk bushes and tufts of salicornia, there lived a very numerous colony of western whip snake.

Not without difficulty – but jealousy makes a man bold, and a woman even more so – Alvise managed to place the pot at the bottom of a little sandy hollow, covering it with branches and earth, though not before having put inside it a dozen frogs, newly sacrificed in the name of the goddess of vengeance, as tasty bait for the unwitting reptiles.

Having set the trap, he awaited the outcome in a boat moored close to the shore. After less than an hour he returned to inspect it: in the pot were entangled at least twenty long, very black snakes circling round in a frenzy, one on top of the other, well fed and visibly annoyed by their overcrowding.

Overcoming his understandable repugnance, the young snake-hunter closed the lid and with his precious slimy cargo rowed vigorously for five hours at a stretch. That is how long it took for a strong and expert rower to reach the remote island of Sant'Ariano from Punta San Giuliano.

He rowed against the current, with his prow pointing northwards, when the tide would have been flowing out of the Lagoon, but he was absolutely determined to be within sight of the convent and to reach it before darkness fell.

The purple *Limonium* was in full flower in the Lagoon; in the orange light of sunset the silvery gleam on the *velme* took on fiery glints. A stirring spectacle of beauty, but Alvise had no eyes for the splendour that surrounded him: hunched over his oars, standing in the stern of his *sandolo*, he rowed with all the fury of betrayed love. He arrived, exhausted, with the last orange ray disappearing behind him towards Lizza Fusina; that brief glimmer of warm light in the already encroaching darkness seemed to him a sign of encouragement, a reward.

He had done it. Now he had only to wait.

After what seemed to him an infinite period of time, in a silence broken only by the intermittent cry of barn owls from the marshes in the direction of Altino and by the disquieting rustle emanating from the pot in the bottom of the boat, the young man finally saw what he was afraid of seeing.

With a feeling only jealousy is capable of inspiring, in which fear of having one's worst suspicions confirmed is inextricably intertwined with the hope they will prove unfounded and lastly a raging desire for revenge, Alvise sighted the gondola of his hated rival, the French gentleman he had surprised only a few days earlier with his unfaithful beloved young nun.

He let the man go ashore and take the short path leading to a side entrance to the convent, via the kitchen pantry, which he well knew to be the most discreet and safest way to reach the nuns' dormitory wing.

After a while he followed after him: in darkness, he crossed the entrance hall beside the store rooms, and holding his breath climbed the stairs that led to the cells, crept along to the little door he knew so well, behind which he could already hear the rapturous whispers of the two lovers in intimate congress.

He had no need even to open the door: between the floor and the door panel, there was a gap of a good few centimetres. He put the uncovered pot near the gap and released into the little chamber of delights the whip snakes, which, given freedom of movement at last, obligingly slipped under the door. He did not wait to see the result: he knew that vengeance is a dish to be eaten cold.

He descended the staircase even more quietly than he had climbed it, set off down the path leading to the landing, his feet barely touching the ground, jumped into the *sandolo*, and rowed and rowed and rowed to the Riva di San Pietro, where he lived.

His act of revenge was a complete success, as soon became known in the City: those twenty black whip snakes did their duty unsparingly. From the cell of the faithless cheat, who in the middle of the night, upon the departure of her strapping Frenchman, found four horrible serpents in the sheets, the whip snakes soon multiplied throughout the convent and within the space of a few months the island, now infested with hundreds of snakes as black as coal and as long as mooring ropes, was abandoned by the terrorised nuns, who were transferred first to Torcello and then permanently relocated to the convent of San Girolamo in the City.

Several attempts were made to clear the deserted island of the infestation, but the snakes on Sant'Ariano resisted every method of clearance, continuing to reproduce vigorously to this very day.

And even now it is not advisable to cross the boundary wall of brick and Istrian stone that surrounds the islet; the whip snakes are not poisonous but they bite – and make no distinction between betrayers and betrayed.

When people say that every place has its own destiny, that is not far from being the truth. And the truth is certainly more fantastic than our imagination, which has tried to find some explanation for the fate of Sant'Ariano, abandoned to the dominion of snakes.

This, it seems to us, would have been sufficient to render that patch of sand and earth in the north-west of the Lagoon if not accursed then certainly a place not to be visited: away from the world, infested by reptiles, forsaken by God and by mankind. Yet even this most far-flung corner of the Lagoon came to have a function once more: the circumspect Signoria of La Serenissima published a decree providing for the transference to that island, from 1665, of "the corpses and ashes occupying those tombs in this City that from time to time are emptied". In other words, the little island of Sant'Ariano became an open-air dumping-ground for skeletons and human remains, a pitifully undistinguished field of bones within the sacred confines of the waters of the Lagoon, long before the Napoleonic decree established the civic cemetery on the island of San Cristoforo.

For a modicum of decency, because La Dominante knew what it was doing then, and the government of the Republic was made up of men who provided and acted for the common good, and not for their own individual interests as is the case today, for decorum's sake and out of respect for the living more than the dead, a boundary wall was erected that year, of bricks and Istrian stone, completely surrounding the island, with a small chapel in the wall granting access to the big open-air cemetery.

Building work that cost the princely sum of one thousand ducats and which was paid for with a contribution from every church, confraternity and monastery in the City.

Over time the bones dumped in that sad spot became so numerous they created a veritable mound that was visible, despite the discreet enclosure wall, from nearby Torcello and even Burano.

The sinister view of that gigantic *memento mori* never blended into the gladdening silver line of the confined Lagoon horizon, but as we know, where man fails nature clearly prevails. Slowly but systematically, therefore, a thick layer of brambles began mercifully to cover the wretched heap, transforming the island into a unique phenomenon in the Lagoon panorama: an unlikely ridge or elevation of land in the middle of the water plain interrupted here and there only by the slender outlines of the bell towers dotted scantily on those confetti sprinklings of earth and sand that constitute the Lagoon archipelago.

It is said that in the very recent past that sinister mound of bones, which would light up with little bluish flames in the Lagoon's dark nights, was visited by aficionados of the macabre or perhaps by medical students who, wanting to see how anatomical theory applied to real models, carried away skulls and other pitiful remains. A stop was put to such practices by sealing off access through the little chapel in the boundary wall.

And as far as we know, the only testimony providing any additional information about Sant'Ariano comes from an extremely inventive and as such not very reliable source: an entertaining short story by Frederick Rolfe, Baron Corvo, in which the unconventional Englishman sets out in his boat with two handsome rowers to discover the far-flung island. The writer relates his encounter with an old fisherman from Burano, the only living witness of what happened in the open-air ossuary a few decades earlier, shortly after the unification of Italy. The old man tells of having taken part in an operation that went on for a whole year, to "evacuate" from the mainland the corpses of fallen soldiers of the Austro-Hungarian Empire, which were polluting the countryside. The remains of the ruling army were treated like waste and unceremoniously dumped in the derelict cemetery of Sant'Ariano. But as everyone knows, the dead take no offence, nor do they claim any right of nationality: Venetians and Germans are white bones of the same ilk, calcium phosphate like the calcium carbonate of seashells beneath the salty sands of Sant'Ariano, a place closed in on itself, covered with brambles, abandoned by mankind, of quintessential loneliness, the most isolated of the islands in the Lagoon.

SANT'ERASMO

Sant'Erasmo, the biggest of the islands in the Lagoon, has always supplied the City with mainly two products of supreme excellence: *castraure* (purple artichokes) and rowing champions. What these two specialties have in common is their character: spiky, honest-to-goodness, strong and combative.

It makes you think that land of sand and salt forges its inhabitants and its artichokes in the same way: with maternal harshness it teaches them resilience, the latter on their upright fibrous stalks and the former on their well-turned wooden oars. Resilience to the salinity of a sui generis humus to produce the most delicious distillation of bitter sap, which makes the *castraure* the most prized of delicacies during the brief and much anticipated first flowering of the plant *Cynara scolymus*, a period usually coinciding with two weeks in the middle of April.

Resilience to the fatigue of rowing against the current, plying the oar with determination to defy every wind (yes, including the dreaded *bora*), applying the wisdom of rowing, of those tremendously ergonomic gestures, the *premar* (exertion of forward pressure on the oar to propel the boat forwards and to the left) and the *stalir* (use of the oar as a rudder to steer the boat), by putting into the water the very least amount of wood necessary, making the most of forward momentum, of the ebb tide. Rowers and *castraure* have come from "Sanrasmo" as precious gifts since time immemorial.

And while the secret behind the panoply of medals and pennants won by the rowing champions of this long island on the margins of the Lagoon extending from the thin sandbar of Lido probably resides in the very remoteness of the place, in its considerable isolation and the consequent need for transportation by the ecological means of strong biceps, the secret behind the excellent taste of those little artichoke buds might lie, if we were prepared to believe it, in a curious and now forgotten story.

Sant'Erasmo has always been the garden of Venice, with Francesco Sansovino already in the sixteenth century writing that the island supplied "the city with a cornucopia of vegetables, and fruit, in great abundance and of excellent quality", and the people who live there, adapting perfectly to their environment, have developed attitudes that reflect the peculiarity of the littoral terrain typical of that strip of salty land; which means they have mixed characteristics that are well suited to the needs of an agricultural life moulded

– or, depending on your point of view, diluted – by marine/Lagoon usages. In short, if we wanted to find in the world of astrological iconography, or better still in the more concrete world of zoology, a symbol that reflects this readiness of the species to adapt, the animal most similar to the inhabitant of Sanrasmo through the ages, an aquatic-terrestrial individual capable of making the most of what this diversified habitat has to offer, that animal would be the crab.

When the Lagoon had not yet undergone the providential modifications to the mouths of the rivers Piave and Sile that debouched into the north-west corner of the Lagoon basin that comprised the dogal territory, the island of Sant'Erasmo, which was then part of the so-called Lido della Mercede, or Lido Albo (because of its light sands), or Bromio (because of the roar of the waves) as Porphyrogenitus refers to it, once had a seaward-facing side; that is to say, it was aligned with the natural axis of the sandbars that extend eastwards from Chioggia in the west, with the barrier strips of Pellestrina-San Pietro in Volta, the Lido and Sant'Erasmo.

And at that time it must have been a wonderful place to live, given that Martial (and we are referring to the great *bon vivant* poet born in Hispania, dedicated, like all poets, to *otium,* certainly a great deal more than to *negotium*) speaks of it as a delightful spot, a commendable retreat, as was the nearby island of Vignole. A site rich in gardens with fertile soil, protected from the mood changes of the restless sea winds by an extensive, cool pine grove that sheltered the villas where the pleasure-seeking inhabitants of glorious nearby Altino vacationed; that same pine grove that during the dogedom of

Paoluccio Anafesto, first doge of the Republic, was designated *Pineta Maggiore*, in reference to the thick wood that graced that sandbar. Undoubtedly, it must have provided a marvellous dark green background on the line of horizon at sea, as conveyed to us by the writer Jacomo Filiasi, an omnivorous reader of ancient documents, who collected early descriptions of the Lagoon: *"And a beautiful prospect (the pine grove) must have given to Venice and formed behind the houses and the vines on the sandbars a tall dark wall, as it were, to the north or the north-east of the vines and orchards."*

If you look at a map of the Lagoon today you can see quite clearly the configuration of the barrier against the sea as a continuous line, interrupted over the course of the millennia by natural events that have led to the fragmentation of the seaboard.

But the perfect conformity between the shapes of one side of the split and of the corresponding side illustrates more clearly than any explanation how the bulge of San Pietro fitted into the indented shoreline of Punta degli Alberoni, just as the curve of San Nicolò follows with geometric precision the western outline of the Sant'Erasmo strip. In short, to put it simply, the Lagoon's defence wall against the sea was like a lonely flat ribbon of desert sand facing the northern reaches of the Adriatic.

We now know that this clear and shallow little sea of ours – the Gulf of Venice – was nothing but land before the long era of melting glaciers led to the flooding of this territory as far as the natural "step" of the Zara-Ancona line, where it gives way to the deeper seabed southwards. So our sandy confines are, in a manner of speaking, recent and their mutations and fragmentations, on the extra-human scale, are events that happened yesterday.

Sant'Erasmo was once hemmed by the sky-blue waters of the Adriatic Sea, with its northern face turned to the salty basins muddied by deposits of earth and detritus carried by two rivers, one vigorously Alpine, the other rising more modestly from the plain. To be more accurate, at the risk of tediousness, it would now seem certain there is in fact a close connection between the two rivers: the Piave, in its middle reach, divided into three branches, the most westerly of which being the one we today call the Sile.

When the hydraulic engineers of La Serenissima, with great expenditure of physical labour, gold coins and ingenuity, turned their attention to the north side of the Lagoon, firstly diverting the lower course of the vigorous Piave and then channelling into its former riverbed the lively and transparent Sile, the longest resurgence river in Europe, the equilibrium of the Lagoon changed radically.

The long crescent of Sant'Erasmo lost its frontline position on the sea, its defensive role partially usurped by the newly reclaimed land of Punta Sabbioni that, as the name clearly suggests, was formed by the accumulation of sand deposits resulting from the modified fluvial-Lagoon dynamics, and by the extensive consolidation works to protect navigation.

A radical change of horizons, geographical and sociological, which certainly did not come about within a few years but at the patient and inexorable pace of the action of water, which does not give much indication on the surface of what its true purposes are but works in secret, tirelessly scouring out, as much as silting up, the floor beneath it, presenting its customary appearance to inattentive eyes, the eyes of land-dwellers.

It does not, however, deceive anyone who has from their very earliest days known, frequented and made use of that azure expanse, frilled here and there with the spume of white horses; anyone who from their own little low-sided wooden craft – be it a *sandolin*, *puparin*, *mascareta* or *s'ciopon* (all variants of the *sandalo*) – is able to distinguish every shade of colouring in the Lagoon floor even through the most opaque of *velme*. A matter of survival, obviously, because depending on the depth of the water one can expect to proceed or else run aground, to catch fish in abundance or come away with empty nets.

One of these expert observers, indeed the most expert – as the inhabitants of Sanrasmo thought of him – was Barba Ciano. Barba Ciano, *tout court*, no surnames on the island, as in any other small closed community; it was, and is, the nickname that determines the identity of an individual, given that the surname is the same for everyone: and for all, of the same ancient stock, along with the baptismal name, there was the epithet, acquired along the way for some physical characteristic or character trait. The epithet in turn became hereditary, serving as a family name. Our Barba – meaning uncle or godfather – was unmarried: in truth, uncle to no one with whom he was directly related, being an only child, but this was a term people once used to include a man of mature years within a family group or community, giving him a title at once respectful and affectionate.

But Barba Ciano had a nickname the islanders used that he was unaware of: *Mazaneta.*

It must have been because of his stocky build, with broad shoulders above a square chest, short legs, bowed like *forcole* (wooden rowlocks), and arms long enough to allow him, with a little effort, even when he remained seated on the *trasto* (transom) in the stern to reach the prow of the *Rente* – his boat, that extension of himself.

It must have been because of the shape of his smooth skull, a cube with prominent occipital bumps, with those two little round black eyes like pinheads, or because of that rolling sailor's walk of his, on a bit of a slant, consisting of rapid spurts and abrupt halts.

He certainly had the skittish, reserved character of the crab, a sort of diffident shyness.

You could not say he was aggressive, but cranky rather, preferring not to have any dealings with his fellow men, but if he did actually have to interact with some human being he would mutter a string of mumbled words in which he would cram the maximum amount of information possible about his state of health, the results of the latest fishing season, and the weather that was on the way. All of which was awash with great quantities of saliva that, not encountering the natural barrier of the incisors, turned into shiny little bubbles resting on his lower lip. Communication was not easy.

And it would be legitimate to wonder whether such a *physique du rôle* was bestowed on him by unkind nature, or whether, as we like to think, adaptation to his environment and the habits associated with his work, or rather his mission, had produced slow but irreversible modifications in our man's physiognomy.

Ciano was a crab catcher and lived on his boat.

He did have a house, to tell the truth, but he dropped by there only fleetingly, two or three times in the season, just to stock up with supplies for his boat, that is to say, a few bottles of wine and some nets or pots, which varied according to the movements of the fish catches of the season. He fished whatever the Lagoon had to offer, a bit of everything, but his speciality, his talent, his passion, his art, was catching crabs.

But let us take a step back and keep our feet on the ground for a moment.

Ciano lived on his boat, moored in a little canal with densely reeded banks that marked the boundary of the big field that was once divided into *ortassa* (large vegetable garden) and *carciofera* (artichoke bed), at the bottom of which, on the south side, stood a little building.

The house, which he had inherited from his father, was constructed of plastered bricks, with walls that were still in good condition, and stone flooring, a few windows without shutters and a door that did not close any more, since about the time Ciano turned thirty, the age when we are entitled to consider ourselves adults and responsible for our own choices. Although in a poor state, it was a proper house and not a hut made of reeds like the Lagoon fishermen's *cason;* a house with a stone hearth and a chimney, a ceiling made of wattle and a great beam of larchwood that came from Cadore when, so his grandfather used to say, La Serenissima had not yet made a pact with the Emperor (in other words, when Ampezzo had not yet been ceded to the imperial crown, so we are talking about 1511). Nonno Ciano – it was customary then, at the cost of clarity, to coin family names in this way – would speak with ill-concealed pride about the improvements made to the house by *his* grandfather, another Ciano, who took advantage – by exercising a certain liberty in purloining building materials by night – of the construction of the circular fort that was erected by the French, treacherous new rulers of Venice, for the defence of the port, around 1810, and which, under Hapsburg rule, the Grand Duke Maximilian had rebuilt, and in which he even took refuge during a noble but no less fruitless insurrection on the part of the Venetians.

The house that belonged to Ciano Mazaneta – thank goodness for nicknames – had seen better years, with people living in it: women who lit the fire under the *cagliera* (cooking pot), worked the land, had dozens of children, men who fished, worked the land, and drank themselves stupid, children who died before the age of three; in a word, happy families. A house full of memories, all the same, constituted of exertion and toil, generation after generation.

It was perhaps this burden of memories that, as soon as Ciano was left orphaned at about the age of twenty, made those four walls intolerable to him: he could not bear living here, he felt too much air around him – at night especially, it was almost as if the walls expanded in the dark, reducing him to nothing – too much space in those rooms that made him feel naked, fragile, defenceless. To fall asleep peacefully, he needed water around him, that rocking motion, the calm sound of the Lagoon's very gentle waves, the damp saltiness of the sea at night. In the early gloom of winter evenings he would wrap himself up in an old dark quilt, salt-hardened like a carapace, and he would stretch out on the *pagioli*, with his head sheltered under the little covering of the prow.

He lived on very little, and that little found room in the

boat; he drank almost no water, preferring *torbolino*, the cloudy juice of fermented grapes that at one time was also produced at his house, fruit of the small vine on the eastern edge of the big field (but Ciano did not work the land, he did not make his own wine, he got it on the island in exchange for small supplies of crab).

As for washing, surrounded as he was by all that dampness the whole time, he was relatively attentive to it: for his so-called personal hygiene he did not really need fresh water – in truth, it was not really fresh, the water that came from the old wells by the house, but *mestizza*, a brackish hybrid: a quick rinse of his face over the side of the *Rente* and at once he felt ready for the day. We all know there is no boat without a name and painted with a large brush in wobbly yellow letters beneath the prow on the starboard side of his was the word "Rente", because it was always *da rente* – that is to say, close by, like a part of his body, a supporting limb, a natural extremity, a wooden husk, a shell.

This extension of Ciano was in fact a *sandalo*, fitted with a removeable cover of wooden planks for stormy days, a kind of rustic, very rustic *felze* (closed cabin for passengers on a gondola) that during the warmer weather he kept onshore, on the bank where he moored the boat, not far from the now abandoned garden that at one time had provided food for his family.

Our man had no inclination for any kind of work other than the scant maintenance of his *sandolo* and crab fishing, least of all working the land, which was too solid, hard, back-breaking and dry – as he would grumble whenever any of the islanders questioned his abandonment of that splendid family field. And so that fertile patch of the island that ran alongside the Canale di Sant'Erasmo – as it still does – right opposite Le Vignole, was left uncultivated no less beneath the August sun than in the January *bora*.

Crab fishing was seasonal, taking place in spring and autumn, which coincided with the most intense periods of agricultural work, so Ciano felt morally absolved in his radical choice in favour of crabs: he had no time or energy left for the land. And anyway, it was clear even if he had wanted to he could not have allowed himself to be distracted from his role as *moecante* (shore-crab fisherman): what with all the little refitting jobs he had to do, repairing the nets and the pots that broke ever more frequently – the Lagoon was not what it once was, with the Lagoon bed tending to silt up with inexplicable rapidity – and mending the jute sacks in which he stowed his catch, there remained few days of idleness even during the "dead" months.

This job, this life, had completely taken hold of him, right from the outset, ever since as a boy he had started going out in the boat with his father to give him a hand collecting the crabs.

They would pull on board the traps crawling with those little creatures, heaped one on top of the other in continuous movement, that tangle of little legs flailing about, and the sound – a sound he had never since put out of his mind – of those bodies scraping against each other.

With swift abrupt gestures his father would empty the contents of the pot into a jute sack that he would tie up tightly with string. But even there, out of sight in the sack, the crabs continued their vain squirming, and in the bottom of the boat that live bundle displayed erratic little moving bulges, emitting a constant suffocated sound.

Then came the most delicate stage of the operation, once the boat was moored.

His father would open the top of the sack on a sloping plank of wood resting inside a big metal tub: the little prisoners would emerge in a frantic jumble, racing along the chute – the *gorna* – with their claws erect, on the defensive. At that point, with amazing speed, his father's big hands would pick out some, just a very few, of those creatures on the march, tossing them into the tub, while the rest were allowed to let their *élan vital* carry them back towards the water.

For Ciano – Cianetto, little Ciano, as he was then – the criteria for selection applied by his father remained mysterious; it took him years of apprenticeship to decipher the fleeting signs that distinguished a *gransio mato* (crab that has already moulted) from a *spiantano* (crab that is about to moult). The *spiantani* placed at the right time in *vieri*, big floating boxes, soon moult, losing their hard outer shell, becoming *moeche*. Despite their name (*moeche* being a feminine gender noun), they are actually male *carcinus asetuarii*, the green crab that march in their millions on the Lagoon floor and on its beaches, becoming that renowned exquisite delicacy at their moment of greatest vulnerability (as the female universe well knows, males become sweeter in relation to their weakness).

Just a few hours are all it takes for the tender *moeca* – that delicious morsel – to turn into a useless leathery *mastruzo* (crab whose exo-skeleton has started to harden), so a close watch and swift action are needed to collect the shell-less peelers at exactly the time when their exo-skeleton is just a soft greenish outer layer.

Ciano had learned so well how to separate the wheat from the chaff that he was also hired by other fishermen on a daily basis at the height of the moulting season; they paid him well – his was a skill that was gradually being lost – but he responded to the day hire requests reluctantly.

Not that he did not like doing this work, even for others, he was generous with his knowledge – a genuine expertise – it was just that he was not at his ease with other human beings and as time went by he had less than ever to do with his fellow men.

He preferred being in his *Rente*, setting his nets, checking the traps: he talked to himself constantly, salivating copiously, mentally counting the *spiantani*, and singing tunelessly to the slow rhythm of the Lagoon undertow, in other words he enjoyed his own company. What was important – indeed, essential – was to be left in peace with his feet well planted on the *pagioli*, preferably moored to a buoy at some distance from the shore.

Money was of little interest to him, just enough to buy tobacco, matches, a few candles when he went to the only shop on the island once every two or three months. For all the rest, for the bare necessities, he found the old bartering system simpler. A bottle of *torbolino* for half a basketful of *moeche*, a few sacks of white polenta in exchange for a bucket of *mazanete*, depending on the time of year.

Because at the right time, that is to say in the autumn, the catch diversifies and the female of our green crab becomes a sought-after prey, full of eggs as red as coral (these crabs are the *mazanete*): delicious crunchy morsels, the perfect accompaniment to a soft polenta.

The truly remarkable event in Ciano's orderly life happened by chance, as is often the case with great scientific discoveries. These days we call this kind of chance *serendipity*.

All Souls' Day had just come to an end, and Ciano had earlier dropped by his house, as he did every year, to light a candle for a while beneath the little shrine with a picture of Sant'Erasmo in the most isolated corner of the kitchen.

That was his way of celebrating the memory of his parents: a private liturgy that he preferred to attending mass or visiting the little cemetery behind the church, both too crowded for his taste.

That night on the boat it was impossible to get warm, the quilt was insufficient to afford him the least cosiness: an unexpected icy *bora* had got up, a light *bora* certainly, because it was not raining and the sky above his crude *felze* was an infinite maze of brightly shining stars, you might almost have been able to touch them, so clear was the deep black moonless sky.

Towards early morning, on the brink of a pallid dawn, he had sensed an anomalous stillness in the little skiff, not so much as the least natural bobbing, the boat was as firm as if it were on dry land: in the unnatural silence of that hour, with difficulty, by the scant greyish light struggling to break through on the seaward side in the east – a rent in the still intensely black sky – he began to distinguish something that had never been seen before. The Lagoon all around had been turned into a white plain: island and water, sandbars and piles were consolidated under a unifying sheet of ice. Friend, mother, cradle and nurturer, the water, now stilled, transformed, indifferent – held his little boat and his life in its frozen grip.

But the man's first thought was not for himself, how to reach safety, how to get back to the shore, instead he thought of the boxes crammed with crabs he had collected the day before, that had been left imprisoned in the frozen surface of the Lagoon: armed with an oar for a hammer, he smashed a small frozen area around the *sandolo*: the solid layer, not being very thick, was soon broken. He freed the *vieri*. Opaque blocks of greenish ice.

The sense of anguish that overcame him at the sight of those hundreds and hundreds of little creatures frozen to death was new and profound. He could not accept their sad and pointless end. Of course it was the fate of those crabs to be eaten, but that was a fair death, inscribed in the laws of the Lagoon, their natural sacrifice, in order to feed people.

Not like this, not because of a treacherous turn in the weather, with the waste of all those clamorous, crawling, still defenceless little lives, without the natural armour of their shells that only a few days later would have protected them. All that energy gone, consumed by the Lagoon's icy maw. For the first time in his life that peaceful and generous place, his liquid home that had always welcomed, supported and nurtured him, that had taught him its mysterious language of salt and beauty – for the first time ever the Lagoon had failed him.

With a sorrow unfamiliar to him he laboriously forged his way through the ice floes surrounding the boat, plunging his oars into the shallows with fury, and moored his boat, tying the rope to the iron ring on the waterfront.

One by one, he unloaded the large woefully silent boxes: he was careful in his movements, because his fingers, numbed by the cold, did not work very well, they could have slipped out of his hands. He placed the containers side by side on the short stone ledge of the embankment, with care, almost with devotion, as if he were following a new liturgy. Every movement cost him pain, in his arms, in his legs, his stiff back had difficulty in bending. Having emptied the boat, he stepped ashore.

He had a clear idea of what to do but he lingered on the bank, surveying the boxes lined up like a chain of small opalescent icebergs. On shore too, the landscape around him was unrecognisable. Every stalk, every branch, even the stones reflected a pale grey light; every detail was sharp and bright to Ciano's moist eyes.

He stamped his feet hard on the slippery ground, to test its grip, to loosen his stiff limbs, then he set about putting his plan into action.

He made that trip, from the bank to the farthest part of the untilled field, five times, loading himself up each time with two boxes under his arms, returning empty-handed and going through the whole process again, with that lop-sided walk of his, all jerks and lurches.

When the waterfront was finally cleared he went by his house, collected the candle stub from the little shrine in the kitchen and then, rummaging under the dilapidated little lean-to at the back of the house, he picked out a rusty shovel, the handle of which was still sturdy, and headed off to the field where he had carried his ten *vieri*.

The shovel penetrated only a few centimetres into the frozen earth but the man was not going to give up: he who had never wanted to work the earth kept at it, his back bent over those indomitable clods of ice and neglect, in the stillness of a bewitched morning. He kept digging and the metallic sound of the blade of the shovel almost bouncing off the ice-encrusted earth set the rhythm for the redoubled intensity and frequency of his strikes. He stopped only when a trench had formed beneath his feet, to the depth of a hand's width and running the whole length of that short side of the field.

The day was almost over but he paid no attention to hunger, tiredness, or the fading light. He then began to empty the boxes into that ditch, gently, slowly: he dropped the little bodies of the *mazanete*, one by one, like little shiny green stones, into the dark furrow from which emanated the warm and welcoming smell of the deep earth; like seeds of a new kind, at once animal and mineral.

Before darkness fell he had refilled the narrow trench with the earth he had dug out, going backwards and forwards, painstakingly stamping down the mound under his clogs to compact the soil.

His final gesture was to stick the stub of candlewax into the top of the furrow and light it, and then with the same match he allowed himself a pipeful of tobacco.

That night he slept in the house for the first time in decades. The bite of the cold during the day had lessened, the water in the Lagoon had slowly melted, but he did not feel up to returning to his boat. There was something weighing on his mind, like a bitter morsel he could not swallow, the betrayal of a pact.

Winter passed as it always did, in the same daily tasks, doing the usual things, repairing the nets, caulking the boat, checking the floats, exactly the same as every year of his life before that night. But inwardly, at the back of his mind, there was that narrow trench in the field, scarcely noticeable from the waterfront, a darker line in the earth.

In March he got some artichoke seed from a neighbour, who was surprised, indeed astounded by this request from someone who had never wanted anything to do with the land, but the neighbour did not seek any explanation and Ciano did not bother to provide any. Those seeds were sown that very day in little holes, made with an embroider's precision, at intervals of one pace in the trench in the untilled field.

In May the young plants did not produce any of the fruit to be expected of a newly planted crop, but they grew with exceptional vitality, forming a grey-green garland on the edge of the otherwise uncultivated field. In September, contrary to all expectation in terms of logic and the natural vegetative cycle – which in any case Ciano knew nothing about – the artichoke bed exploded into a proliferation of firm, swollen, violet flowerheads, like a low stockade.

A genuine spectacle. The islanders could not believe their eyes: they had never seen so fertile an artichoke bed, of such health and abundance.

But not a single artichoke did Ciano harvest: he liked them the way they were, he would go out and check on them every evening before dark, stroking one here, smelling one there. From his boat in the morning, he could see in the distance, beyond the waterfront, that dense rank of violet buds amid the silver-veined dentate foliage, and he had the feeling those *mazanete* had not died in vain, they had returned to life in a different form, not far from the water that had nurtured them.

Since then, and even to this day, the secret of Sant'Erasmo's *Cynara scolymus* remains buried in the island's salty ground, thanks to the little green crabs of the Lagoon, that generous and wise, discreet and fragile mother, forgiven and loved by Ciano to the very end of his peaceful centennial existence.

LIO PICCOLO

As fragile as a piece of lace, as unpredictable as the mood of an adolescent, as changeable as the sky in spring, the Lagoon once had a very different morphology from that we know today.

Certainly a fisherman in the age of Pietro Orsolo I, the sainted doge – we are talking about the tenth century – at the time of the third rebuilding of the church dedicated to San Marco, would have difficulty in finding his bearings in the Lagoon now, the one that today, as we have said, sees the biggest island in the northern Lagoon, Sant'Erasmo, set further back than it used to be from the edge of the open sea, protected from the Adriatic by the Treporti-Cavallino strip of land. Sant'Erasmo was once a barrier island, facing seaward, with its slender beaches confronting the daily assaults of the deep, grey, salty northern Adriatic. Its angry waters, attacking the shores of the little island, all dunes and grassy vegetation, carried away a great quantity of sandy material during coastal storms, making the first few metres of the shoreline dark and torbid like marsh mud. It would take days, after the waters calmed, for all the sand to settle in new strati on the seabed, creating new dunes and depressions all the time, again and again redrawing the underwater landscape like some fanciful artist.

A second-class sea, compared with the azure Mediterranean, yet a dangerous one. This reputation of the upper Adriatic for being a *pelagus infidus* must have been the reason why, perhaps, in their bold and awesome undertakings those extraordinary navigators the Vikings never brought their ships here. They reached the Americas, the Black Sea, they made their way from the Baltic down the great Russian rivers to Novgorod, the Caspian, to Constantinople: it took them two days to go after the Britons; in two weeks they were in Gibraltar; in three, in Greenland. Yet their formidable vessels never floated in the Adriatic beyond the Gargano spur on the Italian boot.

It is reasonable to assume that the treacherousness of that small part of the Adriatic that lies within what used to be called, in a more glorious age than this, the Gulf of Venice – Coronelli has marked on his map of 1688 *"Golfo di Venezia olim Adriaticum"* – all the aggressive force in this pale sea derives almost exclusively from the north-east wind: the *bora*.

A dark *bora* if it brings bad weather – and what bad weather! Such that, from the name of that wind and the damage it causes comes the word *"buriana"*, meaning a great turmoil, everything being turned upside down. On the other hand, the *bora* is a light *bora* if it brings with it the sun and air that is diamond-clear; air that seems to jingle when you look at it in the depth of the horizon, in the thinness of one of those glasses from the Murano furnaces that not surprisingly is called *vetro crystallino* (crystal glass), a sky that appears very high, with that blue ceiling above the pale green floor of the January Lagoon.

Because it is in January that the light *bora* enables the water to appear at its best: it polishes it like an enormous translucent sheet on which a little undulation, the merest ruffle, enhances the chromatic vibration, and it seems that, in the City's little canals and in the silty *ghebi* of the far-reaching Lagoon network, there is, rushing beneath the surface, a current contrary and equal to the *bora*, a fast-moving and sharp water-wind that washes the water, cleans the suspended sediments and makes the liquid perfectly clear, as pure as pure could be.

It is a fair bet that Canaletto's most expansive views – those encompassing the San Marco basin, that linger on a watery foreground as though zoomed in on the surface of this rather cramped version of a greater sea, its waters entering and exiting this stone-built stage set with proprietorial self-confidence – were in fact painted in January, beneath the icy and most clean-cutting blade of the light *bora*.

In any case the Adriatic, which an imaginative poet liked to describe as wild and as green as the pastures of Abruzzo, that wild Adriatic hurled itself, with all its *bora*, upon the narrow beaches of the littoral enclosing the Lagoon to the south.

As we know, the Most Serene Government, in its essential wisdom and foresight but also with a great expenditure of material resources, implemented the deviation of the major watercourses that emptied directly or indirectly into the Lagoon. Among these, and last of all, the Sile, a short and clear-flowing resurgence river, emptying into the north-eastern zone of the Lagoon basin and causing a dangerous and continuous silting-up of the area, was deviated from its natural course and made to flow in the former riverbed of the Piave, which had already been the object of huge hydraulic works previously.

From the end of the eighteenth century the new balanced flow of fresh water, directed towards the Adriatic through this special vestibular maze created by the network of *ghebi* and *velme* and *barene*, actually reconformed the geography of that particular coastal stretch, which until then had defined the boundary between the sea and the Lagoon.

If you compare a sixteenth-century map of that Lagoon area with a present-day map, you will immediately notice the obvious difference in configuration: the advancement of spits of land from east to south-west, the unification of little islets into a single strip extending towards the eastern end of the Lido, the emergence of a new order of terraferma, consisting of dozens of little isolated patches of land previously separated from each other by canals, like fringes woven together into a single entity. The land of Treporti, Cavallino and Jesolo – ancient Equilium – gave birth to new land inhabited by horses of a sturdy race, a collection of fragments that even today can only be reached via a labyrinth of notional roads, narrow dirt tracks lying between fields of water.

Lio Piccolo, one such fragment representing all, soul-stirring in its fragile anatomy of sand and grass, is worth the journey through the tangle of ninety-degree turns that link it to the rest of the world, amid the shimmering mirrors of the shallows and luxuriant clumps of reddish salicornia, sole instance of rubescence in the calming consistency of shades of grey and green.

Lio Piccolo: a name best spoken softly, one of few characters, of few gentle and rounded sounds suggestive of a discreet privacy, a modesty that does not imply paucity but rarification.

For, like a poem, this is a place comprising very little: an open space, more farmyard than piazza; a place of worship, more chapel than parish church; a campanile that is a watchtower, up steep and disconnected flights of steps; and a small palazzo, the vaguely aristocratic air of whose original construction, with a little balcony made of Istrian stone above an arched doorway, calls to mind an old impoverished nobleman wearing a few threadbare remnants of ancient glory.

There was a time when this place, probably an island then, could count on thriving activity as a trading port, linked to the fortunes of the great Altino; it was part of an efficient system of commerce and exchange in the extensive network of the Roman Empire, and evidence of this are the remains that have been found, mostly underwater, of two warehouses, with mosaic flooring.

Already in the Middle Ages our "Little Lido" boasted the presence of two churches, a larger one dedicated to San Salvatore and attached to a monastery, the other named in honour of Santa Maria. Around the fourteenth century a slow depopulation is recorded, and the successive abandonment of the ancient settlement, undoubtedly caused by the deterioration of environmental conditions in the Lagoon and by the consequent worsening of the climate.

It was only towards the end of the seventeenth century and the beginning of the eighteenth that Lio Piccolo came back to life and regained its dignity: the church was rebuilt, and visited by the bishop of Torcello Marco Giustinian, resettlement occurred and cultivation of the land resumed. A Venetian noble family later undertook both the reconstruction of the church – dedicated to the Madonna delle Nevi (of the Snows), as the small stone plaque set in the wall tells us *"Carolus Boldu a fundamentis erexit anno salutis MDCCXCI"* – and the restoration for residential purposes of an earlier seventeenth-century palazzo standing next to the church.

In the nineteenth century the construction of the San Felice saltworks, which were in operation until the early twentieth century, brings to the tiny hamlet a new period of activity. But following this brief spell of prosperity Lio Piccolo too is visited by the same fate of depopulation and abandonment that befalls almost all the islands and peninsulas of the Lagoon, agricultural work is no longer viable, the land is impoverished, the few buildings fall into ruin.

Yet if you manage to reach this tiny spot, which has miraculously escaped the vulgar homogenisation of mass tourism suffered by the seaside resorts nearby, driving or, better still, making your way *"lento pede"* (at a slow walking pace) along the ribbons of green that run between residual pools and Lagoon encroachments, this snippet of perfection will reconcile you with the world.

Lio Piccolo is like a well turned verse: a few essential elements in an apparently simple geometric arrangement, of an acoustic even more than a semantic order: the rhythmic call of the supremely elegant black-winged stilts in their sober black and white livery above two slender legs like twigs of coral, the occasional rarefied cry of the seagull, and the silence of the still but not stagnant water, in rapt contemplation of the sky.

Lio Piccolo is the beginning and the end, the elemental, the core.

You would need only climb, unimpeded, the near-impassable steps of the bell tower/dovecote and acquire the eyes of a fly: to gaze and gaze and gaze. A three-hundred-and-sixty degree view over water, as from the mainmast of a sailing ship; water and a few very green strips of land, if land it may be called: this web of inlay, counterpointing the reflecting mirrors of the Lagoon. It makes you wonder – but you have to be in that very place: *liopiccolo*, so tiny, and all of a piece without any space in between – it makes you wonder whether it is the land that encompasses the water or vice versa, if it is the water that patiently, with its ever deeper caresses, with the quiet passion of wisdom, assembles those spits of land in order to define itself, enhance itself, to challenge the gaze of whoever, from the height of that bell chamber of crumbling brick, might presume to understand, to figure out his bearings, to unravel the shiny tangle of water capillaries and locate his position on the map.

To say the "I am here" that calms the nerves and re-establishes even the most lost self; to become a point, in all its incisive roundness, a modest geometric entity from which all else derives. "I am here" means regaining body, weight, identity, placing oneself rightfully in a space of which one is master.

VENICE NOIR

From that very modest bell tower of Lio Piccolo, the self becomes so small, it disappears.

All around consists of absolute peacefulness, an orderliness independent of you who have climbed those few vertical metres of bricks and mortar; the enigma extending before your eyes cancels out any qualm of rationality, any inclination towards self-affirmation. Quite simply, that whole little universe of water, which expands in the silence, is the reply: and you become what you see.

In the luminous horizontality of the narrowest of channels that wander off into patches of grey-green, in the ghostly manifestations of minuscule strips of mud, immediately colonised by combative vegetation, in the clear understanding of total impermanence, you discover you are part of a beauty without reason, creatural, pre-verbal, pre-gestural, of an absolute and serene gratuitousness that is independent of humankind.

But just before you turn into a tiny yellow patch of lichen on the limestone of the bell chamber, you catch sight of a glint over there, above the horizon.

It is a golden gleam, an arrow stuck in the earth, far away in the distance, so far away you are not sure whether it is a last dazzling ray of sunshine or a frozen flash of lightning. Yet something tells you that distant shape is known to you, its imprint left on you long ago, a silhouette you recognise since forever: undistorted by distance, it retains the outline that matches your oldest recollection of the place you come from, to which you will always belong.

The radius that draws the circumference of La Serenissima,

the gnomon of the Lagoon sundial, the golden angel of San Marco marks the space and the time of a realm that now exists only in the sphere of desire, in History's memory and in the magic circle of the view from the top of the bell tower of Lio Piccolo.

MURANO

There was a time, when the City was shrewd and wise, a time when the precious and already ancient art of glass-blowing – an art that came to the Lagoon from the rich Middle East around the shores of a sea that unites more than it divides, the technical and creative expertise that transforms the human into the divine allowing the alchemical miracle of turning sand into the airy essence of colour – the art of glassmaking kept people and places busy to the great benefit of the Treasury's coffers, in addition to, it goes without saying, the reputation of the Republic of San Marco.

The awe-inspiring workshops with their vats of boiling magma, earthly abodes of portions of the sun, burning concentrations of material pliant to the creative spirit of the master glassblower, brought together a workforce of thousands.

And there were ancillary places, whose purpose was to accommodate wood from the dark forests of Dalmatia and the pale woods of Istria for burning in the great melting furnaces; and silica sand, as white as sea foam, and pink sand that came down the rivers closest to the magnificent Dolomitic peaks, very fine particles of crystal that were once animal life on lands that in a past beyond human memory were all seas.

Gigantic loads of timber in the stoic holds of *trabaccoli* (Adriatic sailing coasters) would cross the treacherous waters of Kvarner Bay, enormous piles of sand in broad straight-sided *peate* (flat-bottomed transport boats) plied their way from the river mouths across the shallow brackish waters of the Lagoon: bustling traffic between land and sea filled the air and animated the wharves of a large island of gardens and villas to the north-east of the City.

Set in the northern part of the Lagoon, easily connected with the mainland by a deep and broad natural canal, the Canale di Tessera, the island of Murano served as a staging post for the transportation of all types of merchandise destined for the well-stocked warehouses of the Queen of the Adriatic.

Of very ancient origin, this place, like others in the northern Lagoon, was inhabited by populations fleeing from Altino, driven out by invading barbarians, and in memory of their nearby abandoned homeland, following an apotropaic and perhaps nostalgic ritual observed in other island-refuges in the Lagoon, this island was given the name of one of the lost Altinese ports: Ammarianum.

As a prosperous trading centre with links to the mainland interior, in particular the marketplaces of Tessera and

Campalto, the new city of Murano could count on its resources of the white gold from the saltworks, located in the northwestern part of the island, in the area where a few centuries later the church of Santa Maria degli Angeli was erected. For it was at the far western end of what was one of the ten little islets in the Murano archipelago, across the broad and winding Canal di San Stefano, that in order to make the most of the natural wealth of brackish water the inhabitants had built out from the shores of the island a long semicircular dam, creating a real artificial lake in which it was possible to optimise the movements of the Lagoon tides and the consequent generous supply of salt deposits.

It was inestimable wealth that lay in the collection, production and trading of salt, when you think that for many centuries the Serenissima enjoyed a monopoly not only of the salt produced in the Lagoon but of that imported by sea from the Adriatic shores of the Venetian domains and even from Sicily, Sardinia and the Balearic Islands.

To protect such a valuable source of income, the Venetian government had from the twelfth century established a judicial authority to oversee the sea salt "*business*" with responsibility for defending their monopoly on supplying the most distant Italian and European states from competition from that other redoubtable producer, the Republic of Ragusa. That proud city, nestled like a pink pearl between the valves of its dazzling thick walls and now called Dubrovnik, could lay claim to the most extensive saltworks of the Adriatic, which occupied little lagoons off the shores of the Sabbioncello (Peljesac) peninsula: the white fortress of Stagno (Ston) and its bountiful white pools for collecting sea salt, each one dedicated to a saint, who, by their constant protection, guaranteed its salubrity and productivity.

Venice and Ragusa were – perhaps not with entirely good grace – resigned to dividing the salt market between them geographically, the former supplying continental Europe to the north and west, and the latter, to the east.

Such a lucrative trade brought into the ever more Serene coffers so much money that in 1428 the Great Council placed responsibility for every aspect of the salt business in the hands of the *Provveditori al Sal* (Salt Superintendants), who had total jurisdiction with the obligation to conduct inspections throughout the realm and the authority to set prices and determine the excise duty payable on the precious white powder (ah, such innocent times!).

At the Punta della Dogana, at the very tip of the *sestiere* (one of the six districts of Venice) of Dorsoduro, looking out over the basin of San Marco, beneath the vigilant eye of the appointed officials, extremely accurate daily logs were kept recording every load that came to the City with the convoys of salt-carrying ships from the remotest corners of the Mediterranean: grain upon grain, huge piles were unloaded from the bursting holds of these vessels and stored beneath the massive trusses of the salt depots that lined the Canale della Giudecca, before being distributed on the international market. So much revenue did this white gold bring in, that in time the *Camera del Sal* (Chamber of the Salt Trade) became a financial body capable of meeting the costs of war, paying off the public debt, lending money to private individuals: powerful and secretive, it operated as a veritable bank.

But let us get back to Murano and to its citizens who, empowered by their ancient origins and by their importance – deriving not solely from the salt trade – to the economy of the State, did not allow themselves to be easily subjugated either by force or by legal means, enjoying respect for their autonomy from the government of the Republic.

The island was, from its earliest beginnings, inhabited by proud and active people, people who did not settle down into the passive role of handmaid to La Dominante but who felt, and who were, just as strong as those who lived in the City of La Serenissima itself.

Thanks to its economic power Murano had acquired exceptional rights: it had its own elected *podestà* (chief magistrate) who together with a Great Council consisting of five hundred Muranese noblemen ruled for the greater good of the island. Furthermore, the island enjoyed the privilege of minting its own coins – the *osella*, a metal substitute for an ancient gift of five *mazorini* (mallards), made by the doge to the noblemen of Venice's Great Council every year on the fourth of December, the feast of Santa Barbara. From 1571, when hunting was banned in the Marano lagoon, the gift in kind was turned into a silver coin equivalent in value to a quarter of a gold ducat. The wise rulers decreed that "…in place of the birds which each of our noblemen was wont to receive from his leader, he should in future receive a coin…", and that the *oselo* (bird) should become a silver coin called the *osela*. The minting of these coins ended on *el tremendo zorno*, that fateful day of the twelfth of May, 1797, and with it ended the whole glorious history of the self-destroyed Republic of San Marco. The Muranese *osella* was only a little shorter-lived, the privilege of minting it having come into effect under the *podestà* Zaccaria Ghisi in 1581, and it bore the inscription *"Munus Comunitati Muriani"*, the coats of arms of the Doge and the Murano *podestà* and the emblem of Murano: a cockerel with a serpent in its beak.

So much weighty tradition, so much islander pride, so much self-respect did not make it an easy task for the wise counsellors of the doge in 1295 to persuade the Muranese to accept the red-hot maws of the glass furnaces on their land when, after a terrible fire, the umpteenth but the most devastating ever, broke out in the City – whose structures at that time were entirely of wood – precisely because of one of those tremendous blazing ovens, a decree was issued that banished all the glassmaking workshops, to be found in every Venetian neighbourhood, far from the extremely crowded fragile City of Venice itself.

Probably the extraordinary concessions the inhabitants of Murano have benefitted from over the centuries originate from that decree: it determined that the site destined to accommodate the dangerous furnaces should be within the confines of the City but outside the bishopric. A decree made to measure, as can be deduced from the fact that the island of Murano, which lay within the bishopric of Torcello, corresponded fully to the requirements: close by but not central; easily reachable from the terraferma for the transport of materials, yet isolated; autonomous but not independent.

The concessions, today we would call it the Special Status, of which Murano self-confidently took full advantage, made it a smaller-scale copy of La Dominante, its more roaring neighbour: palazzi in the flamboyant gothic style sprang up, their tracery built of dazzling white stone from Brač, standing on what was called – more out of pragmatism than emulation – the Grand Canal; these concessions which the cautious government in the Palazzo Ducale kept under strict supervision, seem even to have provided for an unprecedented exception to the hard-and-fast rules governing the Libro d'Oro – the Golden Book.

Since 1319 – after the Great Council Lockout of 1297, which transformed the Republic into an oligarchy, and a few years after the revolt of Baiamonte Tiepolo in 1310, which led to the birth of the Council of Ten – this register had restricted the exercise of power solely to noblemen included in the list compiled by the Public Prosecutors' Office. Such inclusion was allowed only to those who were direct descendants of the Venetian aristocracy and therefore had the right to vote in the Great Council.

These "happy few", males over the age of twenty-five, constituted the nursery in which were cultivated the branches of that oak tree of formidable oligarchic power which governed La Dominante until her sad auto-destruction. The cream of the City, the unconquerable stronghold of political authority and the centre of economic power.

But not all of the Libro d'Oro glittered with the same brightness.

To be inscribed in the register of the powerful was conditional on accepting total control over the personal life of individuals: engagements, marriages and consequent births were ruled by the *dura lex* of élitism. Only four patrician bloodlines could produce a true Venetian of the ruling class, in other words, while clandestine relations with ordinary citizens and the populace were tacitly tolerated, these relationships had to remain strictly childless since the natural issue of an NH (Nobil Homo – nobleman) had to be the fruit of a union – legal or extra-marital – with an ND (Nobil Donna – noblewoman) on pain of being removed from the Libro d'Oro. Here we have the harshness of the Venetian code of conduct which, while it may have had little to do with morality, contributed a great deal to the management of power: the close surveillance, the spying and the denunciations were justified by reasons of state and whoever turned their back on these, carried away by the vain delusion of love, paid the extremely high price of exclusion from the Libro d'Oro.

So it is easy to understand what it might mean to the Venetian aristocracy to have to swallow the bitter pill that the Great Council had, it seemed, ratified – and we can imagine the interminable sitting, the result of endless negotiations and whispered consultations beforehand in Brolo (the garden close to Palazzo Ducale: from which derives the Venetian, and later Italian, word *imbroglio*, a swindle) – by approving the concession whereby the right to be inscribed in the Libro d'Oro would not be withdrawn from noblemen who wanted to marry non-patrician girls as long as they were the daughters of Muranese master glassmakers.

Shocking, but justified by the *ratio* that always governed the decisions of the Venetian administration: the greater good of the Republic. And wherein lay the advantage, in this case, to the Lion of San Marco? What gain could the political establishment see in the co-mingling of patrician blood with Muranese – and, moreover, plebeian – blood?

Averting the brain drain.

In other words, guaranteeing more self-interested devotion to the homeland on the part of the master glassblowers, who with the ever-increasing renown of Murano glass might be tempted – as indeed they were – to betray the secret of its creation, by selling the formulas for the making of special glasses, or, an even more deplorable hypothesis, by fleeing the Republic to find assured riches and work beyond the Alps, where the art of glassmaking sought to compete with Murano, and making available to all the courts of Europe the sophisticated alchemy of the magic material.

What was most keenly desired by foreign rivals were the secret formulas invented by Angelo Barovier that led to the production of the highly prized crystal glass, like pure air shaped into the most sophisticated forms of goblets, wedding cups, *cesendelli* (sanctuary lamps). To the magical transparency of crystal glass was added, some one hundred years later, another precious discovery owed to the mastercraftsmanship of Vincenzo di Angelo del Gallo: the ethereal beauty of diamond-point engraving that transformed household furnishings into gossamer-like lace. The craze for mirrors became such that none of the leading figures of the great aristocracies of Europe would have foregone the contemplation of their own image reflected in the silvery light of a Murano mirror, created from a cylinder of blown crystal glass covered with an amalgam of tin, set in a frame engraved by that top-secret diamond-point method for which Maestro Vincenzo held an exclusive patent.

The glass masters who were prohibited from leaving the City, from opening new glass furnaces, from having contact with foreigners, constituted a veritable élite and not only within the sphere of the island of Murano but throughout the whole City: they were allowed to carry a sword, and they enjoyed, into the bargain, some not inconsiderable immunity from legal proceedings brought by the Republic.

But of all the most coveted privileges, the true object of unequalled desire among the founding citizens, reserved for descendants of the glass masters, the determining factor that could transform a caste of wealthy craftsmen into aristocratic stock – if not of the "first water" – was and remained the right to marry into the nobility. Of course every honour brings with it an onus: a realistic prospect of marrying an NH would also have entailed responsibility and discipline in the conduct of relatives as well as that of the individual concerned. The natural inclinations of a young girl brought up beside the blaze of the furnace, and inflamed by the understandable and natural waywardness of youth, would have had difficulty in following the right course through the Venetian nobility's (apparent) code of conduct, whereby everything was allowed as long as it was hidden behind a mask.

So let us imagine her.

It was 1610 when Cattarina was born, the daughter of glass master Alvise Giandolin, who owned the furnace at number 97 on Fondamenta dei Vetrai. A great talent was that of Maestro Alvise, esteemed in the most illustrious Venetian and foreign palaces: it was not easy to obtain his fanciful wedding cups of milk glass with festoons of zanfirico filigree all around them, thin-stemmed crystal glass goblets with pincered wings of aquamarine, and no matter who commissioned it, they had to wait years to obtain an aventurine plate with mythological figures engraved by his matchless hands. His work was recognisable by the variety of colour, obtained with original formulas with which, it was said, Maestro Giandolin experimented in total secrecy, at night, behind double-locked doors, at his furnace on the ground floor of the small palazzo in which he lived. No one, not even his chief assistant, whom he trusted absolutely, knew the ingredients of the powder mixtures he added to the melt. The little red-leather-covered notebook containing these details was kept in a studded strongbox that Giandolin kept in his bedroom and consulted just before he prepared his mixtures.

The ducats came pouring into the family coffers, enriching the already well-funded dowry of the lovely Cattarina who was becoming a real beauty: the most refined and flawless creation of Muranese magic, with flesh as milky-white as lattimo, avventurina green eyes, tawny-red hair resembling the flames of the glass-melting crucible, and a mouth, a mouth that looked like the best ruby-red glass, the one made with real gold. Hence, the number of suitors for Cattarina's slender little hand, and for the extremely substantial dowry that would have accompanied her, kept increasing year by year, in anticipation of Giandolin's daughter reaching marriageable age.

But of this crowd of hopeful wooers, all of them islanders, a little uncouth, with that indelible mark of slight arrogance typical of the islander, not one in Maestro Alvise's eyes seemed sufficiently worthy of the great good fortune to marry his family's extremely spoiled, true pride and sole joy.

However, in the end what the Maestro wished for his Cattarina came to pass. A highborn suitor presented himself,

Nobil Homo Almorò Moro, whose family had been inscribed in the Libro d'Oro for seven generations, with a palazzo on Rio di Zanipolo overlooking the magnificent facade of the Scuola Grande di San Marco.

A man of unquestionable integrity, the NH had a previous marriage behind him, which had ended tragically with the premature death of his wife, Maddalena Vendramin, who was carried off by a terrible childbed fever at the tender age of nineteen. And the baby that was born in those unhappy circumstances also died, surviving her mother little more than a week.

Almorò had never recovered from this bereavement, surrendering to a grey vortex of despair for decades, losing all interest in life and worldly occupations, including any concern for his modest patrimony consisting of not very extensive farmland at Trepalade in the Duchy's eastern hinterland.

The only relief from the nobleman's dark thoughts came, as from spring water, from fervent prayer, with which Almorò's lips and his heart were afire, as he grieved before the shrine he had installed in the quietest corner of the *portego*, where a miniature of his late wife, painted by an unsure hand but nevertheless a precious token of love from the happy days of their betrothal, was paired with a little school-of-Vivarini painting on a gold background of the "Madonna enthroned with Saints Theodore and Antony the Abbot". The two images glimmered in the deserted palazzo, sparingly illuminated with candles the inconsolable widower personally lighted at matins and extinguished with a sigh after compline.

As the years went by the noble Moro – whom adversity and a continuous attitude of prayer had reduced to the likeness of an old piece of driftwood, grey, bent and gnarled, although he had not yet reached a half century in age – began to find the consolation of peace in regular attendance at the basilica of Santi Giovanni e Paolo, opposite his palazzo, where he took refuge, like a wounded animal in its den, for the service of Nones, and where he would remain until the doorkeeper friar invited him with polite firmness to go home, when the last rays of the setting sun faded from the great stained glass windows of the south transept.

He would spend his days beneath the lofty nave ceiling, alternating between contemplation of the reliquary of Santa Caterina's foot in the prayer altar containing the sacred relic and meditation on death before the altar of Santa Maria Maddalena in the first chapel to the right of the high altar. That great church, the pantheon of the doges, even then contained marvellous treasures of lapidary art and splendid canvases and altarpieces by the most distinguished masters of the long, illustrious period of Venetian colourist painting, and poor Almorò, who no longer had eyes for carnal beauty, was enraptured by the inspired grace of sacred beauty.

Another regular but let us say not entirely enthusiastic worshipper at that same basilica was our Cattarina, who every first Friday of the month was brought by her mother to pray before the foot of the saint whose name she bore, the mother imploring for the advent of an acceptable suitor, the daughter longing for the time to pass quickly so she could escape as soon as possible from that hushed chill and return to the gondola to be rowed through the canals of this City that was all to be discovered, so different from her island in its splendour and thronged with elegant people.

This monthly obligation was the young girl's only opportunity to come into contact with the cosmopolitan world of the great Lagoon City.

In the gondola that took her from Fondamenta dei Vetrai, past the islands of San Michele and San Cristoforo della Pace, and gliding into the broad Canale dei Mendicanti entered the bustling atmosphere of Venice to moor in front of the main entrance of the Basilica di San Zanipolo, Cattarina would quiver with impatience.

She would peek through the gaps in the cabin at the goods-laden boat traffic heading for the San Marco market, preparing herself mentally, with her thirst for life, for the enchantment of seeing the coming and going of men and women on the quayside that ran the length of the Scuola di San Marco, and in the square beneath the towering statue of Bartolomeo Colleoni, and above all on the benches of Salvatore Giacomini's drinking establishment, where many noblemen would gather in circles and sip refreshing drinks while bringing each other up to date on the latest gossip about what was going on in the City, and criticising behind their backs notable passers-by who did not take part in the frenetic tittle-tattle. As Cattarina took those few steps at her mother's side to the great entrance of the church, she was all eyes for the colours, the clothes, the lace, the head-dresses, the necklaces and precious stones, and all ears for the cries, the chit-chat, the murmurings that reached her, like a siren song, from the scattered little groups in front of that marvel of coloured marble which is the facade of the Scuola di San Marco.

The life of the City, with its mysteries and its temptations, emanated a scent that dizzied her. She would have given anything to prolong this feeling that was so intense and rekindled with every visit, each of which was a rare and precious opportunity for her who spent her days in the monotonous quiet of the house on Murano.

For Cattarina, the sole distraction during the interminable hour of devotion in church was a little mirror that her father had created, thinking of her face: a true masterpiece of engraving, with a tiny handle of twisted crystal glass, made especially for the young girl's little hand, perhaps the first example of a pocket mirror.

She was strictly forbidden, however, while in church, to take the precious looking-glass out of its little crimson velvet bag, which the girl wore tied to her belt, because as her mother had solemnly warned her, the mirror is an instrument of the devil, vanity being the daughter of pride, one of the seven mortal sins, and the punishment for that sin of vanity, committed within the sacred walls of the church, could prove dreadful. With its lack of concrete detail, the mother's warning had made little impression on the flighty young girl, who tried to atone for her sin – when she remembered – by adding three Our Fathers, Hail Marys and Glory Be's to her evening prayers.

In truth, Cattarina had never actually looked at herself in the mirror while attending the church service, confining herself to fiddling with the little twisted glass handle until a tiny portion of the reflective surface, just poking out of the velvet bag, caught a ray of light entering through the high windows above the nave and reflected the image of the edge of her blue veil. She knew very well that with just another little movement of her hand she would have been able to see her own image refracted in the silvered crystal; but she stopped herself in time. She liked this challenge, she was tempted by the forbidden and by the frisson of that cold light, like the gentlest of blades cutting across her fingers curled up in her lap. That was enough to distract her from the boredom and the repugnance which that mummified foot, framed by the gold of reliquary, inspired in her every sacrosanct first Friday of the month.

And it was before that very altar of the sainted foot that Almorò and Cattarina crossed paths and their destinies became irrevocably linked.

As often in life, it happened beyond any reasonable expectation: the grey patrician caught a sigh from the glass maestro's daughter at the kneeling stool in front of him, with his eyes he tracked to its source that little breath of air, discovered it came from a young madonna-like profile, marked by two ruby-red lips, framed by a blue Magdalene veil with a small lock of fiery-coloured hair peeping out. And he was inflamed with a sacred love.

The ingenuous representations that, after brief and discreet enquiries as to the identity of the sighing young madonna, the Nobil Homo made to Maestro Giandolin, hit the mark from the moment he presented his elaborate visiting card, engraved in red gold with the crest of the ancient Moro family: a sword embedded in a blackamoor's head.

The negotiations with Maestro Alvise for the betrothal were rapid and to their mutual satisfaction, for to tell the truth the size of Cattarina's dowry was of little concern to the patrician gentleman, who was asking her to join herself to him in the blessed bond of his second marriage because of the profound spirituality of her appearance and not because of the availability of a large share of her family's assets.

They agreed on a simple ceremony, in keeping with the habits of the future groom, something that did not please the young bride. And in truth Cattarina was not particularly happy either with her father's choice: this grey and glum old man did not at all meet the wholesome expectations of Giandolina.

However, the prospect of going to live in his palazzo in the City and the consequent possibility of every day renewing the excitement of being connected with the world, of seeing from the windows of her new home the full flood of Venetian life flow past, the concrete hope, indeed let us say the certainty of joining in and becoming a part of it, revealing herself at last in full flower, alive and full of desires, made sharing her future life with Almorò less disagreeable to her.

Needless to say, all too soon that excitement, that heady scent of discovery, ceased to represent to the married Cattarina sufficient reason to content herself with this husband, a good man, yes, but he bored her to tears, ever faithful to the image of his first wife at home and to the saint's foot in the church, where he continued to spend the best part of every afternoon, and in his unshakeable love and faith compelling the newly-wed bride to accompany him in prayer.

It was just before dusk, with a March sun's last ray still shining, in 1631, after little more than a year of marriage, that Cattarina, exasperated by the unbearable tedium of the second hour of sitting in silence on the usual bench along the wall of the Cappella della Maddalena beside the worthy nobleman absorbed in meditation, drew from the little velvet bag the beautifully decorated little mirror.

This time, however, she did not confine herself to the usual innocent game of capturing the light on the cold silvered surface concealed in her hands: it was a more decisive gesture, the challenge bolder.

Slowly, nonchalantly, holding the twisted handle of the mirror between her fingers, in gloves of the same ruby red as her mouth, she took the little object out of the bag and slipped it between the pages of the prayerbook lying open in her lap. With controlled gracefulness, she raised her hand and rested her cheek upon it, supporting herself with her elbow on the arm of the wooden bench, and looked into the mirror.

From beneath her veil, softly draped over a brow the colour of milkglass, she saw, reflected, confirmation of her own delightful appearance: the eyes looking down towards the mirror caught in their fine avventurina golden flecks the last light of the dying day filtered through the stained glass in the west window; the nose, nostrils slightly flared at the thrill of pleasure, looked even smaller seen from below like this; the vibrant lips relaxed in a barely perceptible smile of satisfaction.

When Almorò roused himself from his final fervent, silent psalm and turned, as he did every day, to his beloved Cattarina to invite her with a little nod to make the sign of the cross together before leaving the chapel – one of those fond and secret gestures that make a couple one in spirit – something in the now already prevailing gloom made him shiver.

How pale his wife was in that attitude of abandon, her face resting on her right hand seemed – was – immobile, as if marvellously sculpted.

He then moved closer, lightly touching her forearm to

waken her, since she had surely dozed off while praying, and at the thought of this, tenderness and reproach for a moment mingled in his heart. She is so young, so lively – he thought – perhaps she needed something else, some distraction, I could take her to pray with the nuns in the church of San Zaccharia.

And as he formed this affectionate plan, he quietly called out to her to waken her from her slumber.

But Cattarina did not stir, so Almorò shook her more purposefully, and as he touched her an icy chill passed from his hand to his heart.

It was no longer flesh that his fingers touched, it was no longer a body; barely distinguishable in the dense gloom was a pale mass, resting against the wall, in the same position as always, that of Cattarina sitting on the bench on the left-hand side of the chapel, yet it was not Cattarina, it was not her body, there remained nothing human in the form that Almorò's despairing eyes perceived in the corner.

Discernible by the light of candles brought in anguished haste by the friars in answer to the nobleman's tormented cry were the perfect features, the splendid figure, the draped clothes, everything that had been Cattarina; but her colouring – the avventurina, the ruby-red, the tawny silk of her hair – had disappeared, transmuted into a uniform marmoreal white.

They kept vigil all night long, Almorò and the friars of the San Zanipolo monastery, praying for her until first light. But not even the pink rays of dawn could alter that absolute pallor: from veil to dainty little shoes, everything had turned into a statue of dazzling white marble.

One detail added to the shock of the metamorphosis a sense of horror and at the same time provided the explanation for what had happened: that magnificent statue, with the head just resting on the right hand, held in the left hand, lying in its lap, a mirror, also of white marble. On the inside of the mirror, the side turned towards the figure that had been so warm and alive, could be seen, neatly carved in the surface not of crystal glass but of black marble, the image of Cattarina's face in the same pose, with the same draped veil, but that sweet face had become a skull with obscene empty eye-sockets and bared teeth.

Cattarina is still there, compelled for all eternity to gaze on an image of death reflected in her mirror, and for anyone who chooses, perhaps not unreasonably, not to believe this story, there remains that marvel of frozen perfection that is the statue resting in an unnatural way against the tomb of the mysterious Cavalier Melchiorre Lancia in the chapel of Santa Maria Maddalena in the Basilica of San Zanipolo.

SAN SECONDO

It requires a great effort of the imagination to believe that behind that little thicket of vegetation, growing wild, all elder and locust trees, laced with ivy and embroidered along its narrow shoreline with broken bottles, plastic bags, and all sorts of driftwood, is hidden a not unimportant trace of the long and varied history of the Lagoon.

One might not even notice it, so undistinguished is its present wretched aspect – that of an open-air rubbish dump, beside the Ponte della Libertà, but one can take advantage of the moderated speed of the train that begins to slow down as soon as it leaves the mainland, where it travels in parallel to a little spit of land projecting towards the City, and where the eye might still be caught by the discreet elegance of a little white construction with an austere columned facade standing at the mouth of the Canal Salso that leads, not without some charm, to the glorious Forte Marghera, a one-time star fort begun by the French, then completed by the Austrians and seized from the Empire by the people of Mestre during the heroic days of 1848.

Next to the last tip of coastland, which became the Venetians' chosen point of access from which to brave the unknown and ultimately forever foreign ways – and a little menacing, too – of the "countryside", that is to say, everything that was not, and is not, the City, there is a little strip of sand and wild vegetation on which in former times stood a customs tower, originally belonging to Treviso, and subsequently to La Serenissima, to whom it was of considerable strategic importance, so much so that it was under the command of a nobleman directly appointed by the Council of Ten. Most of the goods destined for the City came via this place, the boats being forced to go through customs control by a *pallid* (palisade) that directed them this way, and this way, too, came merchants and visitors travelling down from the lands to the north. Here, beside the customs tower, there stood what was originally a Franciscan monastery, then became a convent for observant nuns, dedicated to San Giuliano di Buonalbergo, which provided a safe refuge for boats caught out by the Lagoon's bad weather, no less unexpected than dangerous, especially when the gusty bora raged: strong squalls that put in jeopardy small Lagoon craft, despite the shallow waters. This convent suffered the same fate as so many other religious houses in the Lagoon, first ending up deserted, and before long destroyed, so that today nothing remains of San Giuliano as it once appeared, not even that view of San Giuliano with the tower and boat shelter that Canaletto painted, a work last heard of in Berlin in 1945, and which perhaps like many other masterpieces is today locked away in the vault of some obsessive collector for his own exclusive pleasure.

But let us stay on our train that is travelling at walking pace across the Ponte della Libertà.

And let us stay here on the bridge – something that happens irrespective of our will, given that the trains frequently stop on this stretch of the railway across the Lagoon because of the signal lights in Santa Lucia station. We can take the opportunity to reflect on what allows us to cross the Lagoon and reach the City without having to take to the water.

This bridge – that at the time of its construction raised so much controversy among Venetians worried about the future of their City, which would be relinquishing for ever its splendid isolation – was built at the behest of the Austrians in a very short space of time, given the technology of the period and the difficulties of building on mud. When Archduke Rainer, Viceroy of the Kingdom of Lombardy-Venetia, laid the first stone on 25 April 1841, the spirits of the oppressed Venetians were not raised in a paean of joy at the sight of their once Most Serene and now Most Wretched City yoked even more firmly to the Austrian wagon. The short-sighted citizens did not marvel at the technological achievement of the Lombardo Veneto Railway Company that sank the first of 75 thousand wooden piles on 10 May 1841 and the last on 25 September 1845, in addition to the 100 thousand planks of larchwood from Cadore and 150 thousand thousand (sic!) blocks of Istrian stone and 23 million Treviso bricks. Short-sighted and unaware of what would be happening some one hundred and sixty years later not far away, in front of the harbour mouths into their Lagoon, they complained in whispers – their Imperial rulers did not tolerate dissent – and suffered the technological wonder as an injustice. Who knows whether the Lombardo Veneto Railway Company paid any kickbacks to engineer A. Noale, director of works, or to Antonio Busetto, known as Petich, the contractor; what is certain is that it cost six million Austrian lire and in a little over four years the 3,603-metre long, 9-metre wide bridge was standing firmly (as it still does) on its arches.

Our reflections on the difference between then and now, between that Hapsburg construction and the incomplete behemoth with the biblical acronym and the disgusting malpractices accompanying it, are interrupted.[2] Our train is off again, resuming its slow progress towards the City.

With bitter Mosaic recriminations weighing on our mind, we turn our eyes eastwards, settling our gaze on the shimmering backdrop behind the northern Lagoon, crowned on clear days with the blue circle of the Friulian Alps, and our bitterness fortunately dissipates.

At a distance of some one hundred metres from a low rampart beside the bridge with a parapet of white Brac stone, our eyes fall on a little green patch strewn with rubbish, lying between the bridge and the Canale di San Secondo, which is as busy now as in the past because it is deep and wide, a broad aquatic expressway providing a northern link between the rest of the world and the City.

That little green patch is the island of San Secondo, and it

---
2 See footnote on page 14.

is there we would like to stop for a few moments in imagination – because it is not otherwise accessible – to recall the story of this one small tessera in the great Lagoon mosaic.

Not even saints have been spared from the healthy pragmatism of Venetian mercantilism. Just think of poor San Teodoro who after years of honourable service found himself robbed of the title of patron of the City by the newcomer San Marco, so there was nothing better left for him to do than perch on that tall column with his crocodile under the close watch of the nearby lion. The Venetians did not waste much time in reducing a sainted protector to second rank in order to take refuge under the sheltering wing of another, more powerful or effective Christian martyr, exactly as happens even today, and not only in this City, with regard to other more secular and more nefarious forms of protection.

But let us look at the islet of San Secondo: there was a time, in the very distant past, when it was named after Sant'Erasmo, bishop and martyr, tortured, beaten, covered with pitch, boiled in a cauldron and it seems (although there is no corroborating evidence for this) also disembowelled – in 303, in the age of Diocletian, they did nothing by halves.

Erasmo being the protector of seamen (and invoked against stomach ailments, but that is irrelevant), an image of the saint – also known as Sant' Elmo, who gives his name to the famous fire – housed in a modest wooden shrine on a pole near the island's beach, continued to protect sailors and keep them safe in the dangerous and deep canal of which we have spoken above.

It was, if not exactly the dawn of La Serenissima's history, during the early hours at least, when the Venetian Baffo family, probably for intercessionary prayers answered, replaced the rickety wooden structure protecting the tortured martyr with a little church of stone and brick. It was 1034, not long after the feared millenium had passed, and in short beside the little church of Sant'Erasmo an unassuming convent was established for nuns of a Benedictine order. The island's poverty was such that Doge Vitale Faliero – the first doge of Dalmatia and Croatia – assigned the holy place some modest annual revenue. We are familiar with the harshness and rigours of those so-called dark centuries of the Middle Ages, a period of strict religious observance, yet riven with schism, heresy, tumult; in the City, still a work in progress but already focused on its own power, aware of its exceptional position in the geopolitics of the century, torn between the philo-byzantine faction and the philo-germanic, a group-controlled administration of political power began to emerge: to collaborate with the doge, and thereby avoid any possibility of absolute monarchy, there were elected councillors, the future Minor Council.

The convent on San Secondo fulfilled the role of a travellers' refuge, hospitality being the sole absolute and indisputable law of the sea. But the Benedictine nuns' cordial welcome was not always repaid with gratitude: the ancient chronicles relate that in 1099 Bonio – do not be misled by the name – official representative of the bishop of Treviso (and acting on his behalf?), having come to the island caused serious damage to the convent; but he did not get away with it: he was captured and imprisoned by the wise doge Ordelafo Falier.

We come to the fateful year 1237: the abbess at that time

was Donna Florigentia, when Pietro Tiepolo, son of Doge Jacopo, having conquered the city of Asti, took possession of the body of San Secondo, former patrician, bishop and defender of the city against the Lombards, and brought the sacred relic to Venice.

But his laudable enterprise was not entirely successful.

The story goes that the boat with the sacred remains tried numerous times to cross the northern Lagoon to deliver the saint's body – *"The body, still intact apart from the nose, lips, ears, tongue, is authentic... because the Venetians, being extremely cautious in all things, no matter how small, would not be deceived, least of all in this"* – to the church of San Geremia. But after various strenuous attempts to pass the island then known as Sant'Erasmo, despite the efforts of the *"remorchianti"* (rowers of the tow boat), the sea became calm only when the chest containing the precious treasure of the saint's body was put ashore. Nor did the heavens stop at that, in making clear it was intended that San Secondo should remain on the island: indeed, while they were unloading the chest containing the saint a corner of the reliquary touched the fresh water well that stood in the courtyard between the guest quarters and the church, and which had run dry some time ago; and instantly, miraculously, it produced the sweetest fresh water. While the nuns and generous Venetian benefactors were seeing to the preparation of a place worthy of the saintliness of the miracle-working body, a nobleman from Asti is said to have come to the island with the undeclared intention of satisfying local pride by reclaiming the sacred remains, but it being obviously impossible to abduct the whole body in order to return it to the saint's native city, he contented himself with cutting off a toe, so as to take back to Asti at least a part of its patron saint; but on his return the would-be abductor could no longer find the relic, which in the meantime had miraculously and independently rejoined the body on the Lagoon island, where it remained for centuries, a copper band indicating where the stolen toe was reattached.

Indubitable heavenly signs identify the island as a place favoured and blessed by the saint of Asti; so inevitably Sant'Erasmo is dismissed and San Secondo with good reason is named in his place as eponymous saint of this small territory in the Lagoon.

Perhaps because of the benevolent influence of the saint's remains or because of favourable conditions in the north Lagoon, the fishing in that area was truly miraculous: the chronicler tells us that the waters surrounding our island were thronged with boats using various methods of fishing – *"with ring net, seine net, fyke net, drift net, trammel net, cast net, hand line, drag line, trawler baskets and multi-pronged harpoon"* – and that there, *"they go after fish and molluscs at all hours and they catch grey mullet, rock goby, flounder, sea bass, turbot, eel, elvers, oysters, prawns, shore crab, various clams, autumn crab, soft-shelled crab and shrimp in great quantity, but the flounder, clams and oysters of San Secondo, having good fat feeding grounds around them, have the advantage in the market place."* But not only was the sea generous to San Secondo; indeed we know that during those centuries the island was rather larger than may be seen today – more than twice its present-day extent – and famous for its climate and vegetation, able to boast of *"a belvedere hill, vegetable gardens and gardens big enough to stroll in"* and even a little laurel grove. The list of plants that grow there is wonderful, some self-sown, others cultivated, whose fanciful names create a delightful tableau of sound and a miniature Eden, which we would like to present – as with the information above – in the words of our chronicler, the Dominican prior Domenico Codagli da Orziuovi, who, in 1609, from his little island, wrote: *"...there are pergola grapes of every kind of the most delicate flavour, but the Brunesta, Giubebo, Marina, white and black Muscat and Marzemino are most excellent. Pears, apples, quinces, apricots, peaches, mirabelles, plums of every sort, sloes, figs, blackberries, almonds, jujubes, olives, hazel nuts, gooseberries, and sorb-apples I have seen there... I leave aside the common trees, willow, poplar, tree ivy, elder... but come to the noble plants, the cypress, which the Ancients say was sacred to Pluto, god of the underworld, a tree not native to Italy... the laurel, myrtle, box, pomegranate, euonymus and persimmon, greatly celebrated by Theophrastus and Pliny... rosemary grows wonderfully well there. Every kind of native and foreign flower, tulips, sincadami, hyacinths and other unusual and beautiful flowers... a species of pale blue jasmine that self-propagates... poppies of every kind, tree mallow, saxifrage, plantains, costmary, celandine, dragon aurum, spikenard, dill, iris, sempervivum, St John's wort, ivy, oleander, maidenhair fern, and reguaritia and mandragora have also been seen there."*

A garden of delights to be used for culinary purposes and for the pleasure of the monks and visitors taking a stroll. On the renamed island, thanks to generous donations made by noble families from Venice and the mainland, the nuns under the leadership of energetic and enterprising abbesses enjoy a comfortable and rather pleasant life, as did many of the convents in the Lagoon.

There must have been a great amount of coming and going on the shores of San Secondo, since the renown of the convent soon exceeded the holiness of the place, whose doors were left open to the pleasure-seeking Venetian aristocracy. In all honesty, and in fairness to the nuns, it has to be said that the beginning of the sixteenth century had seen the serenity of La Serenissima in great jeopardy, imperilled by the deadly alliance of the League of Cambrai, promoted by Pope Julius II: the world against Venice. In those years the maritime republic had been crushed and troops of the Holy Roman Empire had made inroads to the very margins of the Lagoon, occupying towns and countryside, and sniping at the islands from the Lagoon perimeter. So there were the poor nuns on the island of San Secondo, exposed to attacks from the mainland; with the enemy at the gates, every day could have been their last, they were bound to take advantage of a few carnal pleasures.

And indeed, as our honest chronicler reports, in 1515 – when the dreaded League was actually fractured but the Empire's intentions were still rapacious and menacing – the island found itself in serious danger, with a number of powerful guns, placed on the northern edge of the Lagoon, directed against the City. San Secondo lay in the line of fire, but the fearless nuns did not abandon the island, taking refuge in the shrine of their guardian saint, who in his utmost benevolence thwarted no less than ten large pieces of artillery, safeguarding his own remains as well as the Benedictine community that judged by moral standards would not have merited such indulgence. But as we know, saints are generous and well aware of the weakness of the flesh; unlike the vigilant government of the Most Serene Republic, which in 1519 took the irrevocable step of closing down the convent, thereby replicating the fate of many other religious retreats in the Lagoon, after an unsuccessful attempt at "rehabilitation" of the place with young nuns from the Observant convent of Santi Cosmo e Damiano on the Giudecca.

The island was subsequently left uninhabited, subject to the depredations of *"ruffians and fishermen"*, until in 1533-4 a group of Dominican friars settled there, led by *"Father Zacharia Lunense from Lucca, of the Dominican Observance, who was loved and respected in Venice"*, who brought radical improvements to the little that remained intact of the two hectares of land under the patronage of the saint of Asti. But in 1539, right in the middle of the restoration sponsored by the Senate of La Serenissima to the tune of two hundred and fifty ducats a year, *"a priest of the Venetian Patriarchate"*, for motives that have never been made clear, started a fire on the island. Along with some precious polychrome flooring, capitals and marbles, also destroyed in the fire was an altarpiece of the Most Holy Rosary by Giovanni Bellini – something that still pains us.

For decades, chronicles of the City were to tell of another more ruinous fire: it happened on the night of 13-14 September, 1569, when gunpowder stored in the Arsenal exploded; the explosion and the subsequent vibrations were such that the entire City trembled, and the whole area of Celestia suffered a huge amount of damage.

This was what prompted the Senate to relocate its munitions stores on to islands, erecting defensive towers for this purpose, the first example of which was built on San Secondo, the Torrione dei Marmori – that little square tower standing on the eastern perimeter, which was restructured during those years, along with new quarters for the *Hospitaria*, the dormitory rooms, and the portico connecting the convent to the church. And there in the church occurred the umpteenth miracle performed by that munificent Asti saint, who in the terrible fire that devastated the building, saw to it that two huge roof trusses fell in such a way that the beams interlocked, one on top of the other, right above the chest containing his relics, thereby protecting his own shrine from further collapses of the building and the destruction of his own shrine.

Henri III, King of France had recently passed through Venice, in July 1574, on his way from Poland to Paris, where he was to be enthroned after the sudden death of his brother Charles IX: the Bucintoro, *"and a great many people in gondolas decorated with gold brocade and velvets of different colours"*, sailed in a great procession by the island of San Secondo. By order of the Signoria the island fortress was to deck itself in full regalia to welcome the illustrious guest: *"To the sound of trumpets and drums, from the windows and walls of that sacred temple, and all over the island, hung silk pennants, standards and flags of various kinds."* So it was only a few months later, less than a year after that day of great festivity on the island, that the protection of San Secondo failed, alas, to prevent the outbreak of plague, an indirect consequence of the wars against the Turks. Despite the reassurances of the Padovan doctors who declared the disease to be non-contagious (!), it killed seventy thousand people over two years, including the genius Titian, who was in truth already more than advanced in years. The government tried to contain the disease by removing the sick to the islands of Lazzaretto Vecchio and the larger Lazzaretto Nuovo; but other places of quarantine were needed to cope with the crisis, so after the friars had been placed in safety in San Domenico and Santa Croce the island of San Secondo was turned over to victims of the plague.

There followed another period of decline for our little island, which must have been in a really bad way if the friars, after an initial inspection, refused to move back there. But as we know, the government of the Republic knew just how to persuade the preaching brothers to return: the threat of handing over the island to another monastic order meant that the Dominicans resumed their monastic life there and restoration works were subsequently carried out.

Now, rather than get lost in details of other minor miracles (deflected lightning strikes, women rescued from storms, etc.), we will conclude our sojourn on this little island of fragrant gardens with a last charming gesture of benevolence on the part of the protective saint, as conveyed to us by that diligent and honest chronicler the above-cited prior: the miracle of the Giacciolo Pear Tree. The location is one of the orchards within the precincts of the convent, the season probably still unpropitious: *"...So, gathered round the table under the shade of this tree were Pre Facino, now rector of San' Apollinare, Gioan Alberto de la Fortuna, and many others, at a time when ripe fruit could not be expected of this tree, and while they were arguing about this impossibility, one of them said the Saint could make the tree yield ripe fruit, and he had no sooner uttered those words than to the amazement of all, without the intervention of any human being, there fell from the tree the freshest and ripest of pears, which they all enjoyed with the utmost pleasure, and accusing each other of irreverence they agreed to repave the church in memory of this abundance."*

Bear in mind this miraculous Giacciolo Pear Tree for the few more lines needed to give a brief resumé of the rest of the island's sad story...

The Dominicans remained on San Secondo until 1806 when, following the edict that ordered the closure of more than thirty of Venice's convents and monasteries, they were transferred to the convent of the Gesuati on the Zattere, together with the saint's remains; the island passed into the clutches of the Napoleonic navy that soon ended up – as in so many parts of the City – destroying and pillaging all the fine things that had been created in almost one thousand years of history. It became a military base, first French and then Austrian: the shoreline was consolidated, the perimeter, the contours were modified, the boundaries altered. Nothing was as it had been. The little isle briefly became a Resistance outpost during the 1848-9 uprising: that was the last gasp of a typically Venetian story.

Decay and neglect are now the only laws that prevail on San Secondo.

But... if you are on that train that slows down on the Ponte della Libertà in early spring, at the end of March or during the first days of April, look out, above and beyond the thicket of ivy and locust trees and elder bushes run wild. It will not be difficult to pick out in the midst of the dark greenery a big patch of white, like a cloud sitting right on top of that plot of land, like foam from the Lagoon mysteriously frozen in a graceful explosion a few metres above sea level. What you will be seeing is the last wonderful small gesture of affection that San Secondo is making to his island: it is the Giacciolo Pear Tree that flowers every spring.

To San Secondo

Against you, who calm the sea, still the winds:
Cure the sick, and free the possessed;
Scourge of souls condemned
To hell, to suffer pain and torment.
Already, all Pluto's dominions have risen in protest,
Upbraiding Heaven with loud complaint,
That a Knight of the order of the golden spur
Should oppose them, a shield to the people.
By contrast the guardians of the gates of hell,
Full of fear, Lucifer defends,
And Cerberus hides, and Satan flees.
This the dreadful chambers, the Monsters, and Death know,
That to the amazement of all nature
At the sound of your name, hell groans.

(Sonnet by Padre Domenico Codagli da Orzinuovi, cherished author of *Historia dell'isola e Monasterio di San Secondo di Venetia*, published in 1609 by Francesco Rampazetto Editore.)

POVEGLIA

Blessed friars! Blessed nuns!

If the islands of the Lagoon had not been hospitable places of hermitage, at least in the intentions of the founders of the numerous monastic establishments across those waters, the island geography surrounding the City would be quite different.

Sadly, as we know, for the majority of these sites of spiritual retreat, there remains only the historical account, the written testimony in the rich and detailed chronicles of La Serenissima, since any monumental and architectural remains mostly have been "removed" during the long centuries of abandonment, starting with the fatal Napoleonic edict that emptied and suppressed the monastic institutions of the new

Empire, and ending up with the present-day period of looting with impunity and of often artfully engineered neglect.

To tell the truth, even some time before the fateful French intervention various vicissitudes and questionable morality had led the ecclesiastical authorities, but more importantly the watchful and prudent government of La Serenissima, to make sudden transfers and consequent reassignments of these holy places to new custodians, who offered greater assurance of faithfulness to the rules of monasticism, sometimes with totally disappointing results.

We will not try to analyse the reasons for so little inclination to observe the strict rule with any degree of zeal, but the economic need to protect family patrimonies, without dividing them up and consuming them in dowries, made common the unwelcome imposition of the monastic life on younger sons and daughters of the Venetian aristocracy, who by nature would have justly aspired to a very different life. So it is easy to understand why those unwilling cenobites should succumb to worldly temptations.

The fact remains that in the secular Republic, the convents scattered across the archipelago were assigned a duty of offering hospitality that went beyond the usual monastic welcome extended to the pilgrim, being invested with a certain political aura, as a kind of outpost in the complex and delicate geography of San Marco's diplomatic machine.

Nevertheless, some islands in the Lagoon – but they really can be counted on the fingers of one hand – can boast of a more "secular" history that, while not totally ruling out some settlement related to religious orders, does not see the fundamental shape of its own history marked out by the walled

– though not inaccessible – perimeters of monastic life.

In terms of logistic importance, because of its relative proximity to the centre of the City, Poveglia has carved out for itself in the millennial unfolding of Venice's island history a position of great importance: such is the defensive value of this island that the few in number but still proud native population are fighting a determined battle to restore to Poveglia its due dignity and to the City a precious tessera in its extensive mosaic.

Lying alongside the Malamocco canal, ancient Pompilia – of uncertain etymology, but perhaps deriving from *pioppo*, meaning poplar tree, or from Via Popilia, the Roman road built at the instigation of the consul Popillius Laenas, linking Rimini with Aquileia – marks the bifurcation of the waterway from the Malamocco port entrance, where it splits into the two canals, Poveglia to the west, and Santo Spirito, which then becomes Canal dell' Orfano, to the north.

The first known settlement dates back to 421, when Padovani and Atestini fleeing from the barbaric invasions took refuge on the island, which was big enough to guarantee the development of a community that soon became significant in terms of numbers and organisation, even equipped with defensive walls and a castle.

Four centuries later, it was the turn of the Franks, with Pepin, who came to disturb the peace of the former Padovani-Atestini, now happily settled "Povegliotti", who did their utmost to defend the Lagoon from the northern intruders, but in the end were obliged to withdraw to the more secure, inner Realtine islands.

Poveglia was then left deserted for a few decades, but in

864 a "coup" – at that time called a conspiracy but the intention and procedure remain the same – upset the fragile equilibrium of a tumultuous period for La Serenissima, engaged in a defensive struggle against Saracen pirates, and also others, culminating in the defeat of Sansego (present-day Susak, a charming little island not far from Lošijn, which if geography allowed would merit a little chapter of its own in these pages), but then concluded with the Pactum Lotharii, which recognised Venice as a duchy with sovereignty over the Lagoon wetland area, what would become the future city-state and its Adriatic coastal possessions. In those difficult circumstances the seditious spirit of some families, involved in *"constant avid intrigue for power"*, gathered round the unpopular figure of Doge Pietro Tradonico, supported in government by his son Giovanni, as co-regent. When the latter died, *"the odious tyranny of his impertinent and quarrelsome retinue"* sparked the outbreak of violence and it was Doge Pietro himself who paid the price: he attended vespers at the church of San Zaccaria on the eve of the celebration of the Holy Cross and was attacked outside the church and slain. The conspiracy brought disorder and instability for about two months, at the end of which Orso was elected – the sources assert and deny that he was a member of the Partecipazio family – an excellent doge from his very first acts of pacification: he condemned to exile those who had played any part in the conspiracy and removed the hot-headed partisans of the assassinated doge (who had barricaded themselves in the Palazzo) to the island of Poveglia, granting them generous payments and privileges.

So we come back to our island, now repopulated with a

group of one-time desperados, placated with extraordinary concessions.

Happily, the warrior spirit that roared in the new inhabitants of the island were channelled into less aggressive and more profitable activities, so much so that within a few decades the newly settled community managed to populate the place with more than two hundred families, living in some eight hundred dwellings, with an abundance of vines and precious saltworks to rely on. The concessions they had been granted by the doge meant they were exempt from paying taxes and from military service – save in exceptional cases of war under the command of the doge in person. It is curious, that "direct" relationship between the Povegliotti and the doge over the centuries: it was established from the time of Doge Orso that as a sign of their loyalty (the spectre of sedition always hovered over the island) a delegation of seventeen notables of the Poveglia community should pay homage to the Serenissimo Prince on the Third Sunday of Easter, taking part in a banquet. The *mariegola* (statutory regulations) of the confraternity of San Vitale, titular saint of the church on the island, describes the strange ceremony that took place between the doge and the delegates, reporting the few but important exchanges of dialogue in the strictly codified ritual: *"God give you good day, Doge, we have come to dine with you."* Then the doge would reply: *"You are welcome!"* and the seventeen (we do not know whether in unison or with one speaking for all) would say: *"We seek a favour."* Then the doge: *"Gladly. What is it to be?"* And the Poveglian reply: *"We would give a kiss."* At that point every one of the seventeen would kiss the Prince *"on the mouth"*, and having completed the courteous demonstrations of affection, they would then all go and dine together in the doge's antechamber. The dogal kisses would bring to the civic coffers *"26 lire de picoli"* (one of two currencies used in Venice, the *picolo* contained less silver than the *grosso*), – it is difficult to determine the value in present-day terms – but more importantly, confirmation of obedience to La Serenissima's authority.

Another moment of "intimacy" with the doge was reserved for the Povegliotti when the Serenissimo Prince went in procession from the Palazzo to the Bucintoro, moored in front of the Piazzetta, for the marriage with the sea ceremony, on which occasion a group of islanders – we like to think of them as burly and intimidating – acted as a "bodyguard" at the doge's right hand.

But apart from these symbolic privileges, of rather greater significance, it seems to us, were the fish-trading rights enjoyed by older – over seventy years of age – Povegliotti, who could buy at a fixed price fish from the bounteous Istrian waters and then sell it on, probably at a much higher price, at the San Marco market (which, for anyone who might not remember, used to be located more or less where today we see the Giardinetti Reali).

And finally, a clear indication of the contractual power of the Povegliotti was that the doge had granted to them, and to them alone, the licence to tow ships in the Lagoon basin.

The monopoly, which provided for the *remurchi* (tow-boats) to take charge of the vessels at the port of Malamocco – the entrance to the Lagoon – supply the rope, tow the vessels on a line, and moor them at the quayside, was no small matter.

It should be noted that the entrance route into the San

Marco basin was not easy or without danger, since the canal leading from the port of Malamocco into the basin was tortuous and shallow, scattered with submerged obstacles, in short, only for experienced navigators with expert knowledge of the local hazards. That very canal proved fatal to the French in their attempted attack on the City, in that above-mentioned incident when the inhabitants of Poveglia distinguished themselves by their courage and their skill; apparently the name of the so-called Canale "dell' Orfano" derives from that naval engagement, in which a great many perished in those treacherous waters, leaving many children orphaned, waters that certainly in the dim and distant era of Lagoon migrations, were the favoured arena for violent conflicts between the island populations and those of the littoral.

So, these exceptional rowers – we have already conjectured that the Povegliotti were of extremely muscular build – under the command of a pilot who was responsible for the delicate operation of towing, would man sturdy vessels with broad hulls and shallow drafts, capable of manoeuvring with ease in the sandy shallows.

Legend has it that the shrewd Povegliotti, to increase their income, had strewn the route with submerged obstacles – specifically, palisades with sharpened tips, whose underwater location only they knew – so as to make access to the basin impossible, and anyone who unwisely failed to engage the services of the *remurchianti* (rowers in the tow-boat) paying the penalty of having the hull of their ship gashed.

One rower in particular stood out for his courage and his vigour, a man who was all muscle and nerves, a loner and an introvert by nature, without family and without a name, who had washed up on the island during a serious squall, a storm that came with hailstones and a tornado so violent that more than half the houses had their roofs blown off, their doors torn away, and animals and farm equipment were sucked up by the furious whirlwind. That part of the inner Lagoon is a confluence point where strong winds and contrary currents intersect, a kind of funnel for tornadoes and storms, that even today is a worry for Lagoon navigation.

In the unreal calm that followed the disaster, amid the ravaged vegetable gardens and vines and the daunted bewilderment of the nevertheless indomitable Povegliotti who, emerging from their devastated houses, almost weeping, bewailed the damage and the terror, each claiming to have suffered worse losses than the other; against the brief line of the Lagoon horizon visible from the southern shore, looking towards Malamocco, already light again and quite tranquil and clear as only after the strong rainstorms that cleanse the air and refresh the still waters of the inner Lagoon, there appeared a giant, naked and staggering, for all that his legs were sturdy.

He walked slowly, with an unnaturally rigid posture, his head held high, his extremely dark eyes turned towards the few islanders who were gathering up from around the houses their scattered belongings.

Those who saw him first say he did not seem human, he looked more like a sea creature, dark and glistening with water and reddish seaweed, his arms held close to his torso, his fists clenched, with thick tawny hair and a long beard that came down to his chest framing a gaunt face with prominent cheekbones.

The islanders warily tried to question him when, later,

after being restored with some bread and a bowl of wine, the man had somewhat recovered, and the hallucinated gaze had gone from those deep, deep brown eyes; but it was no good, they could not get a single comprehensible word out of him: hard guttural sounds, as jagged as broken glass, issued from his mouth. The steward of the community, in an extraordinary meeting of all the heads of households, inferred from the stranger's slow, broad gestures that he came from the Orient and had been shipwrecked off the Lido, and had reached Poveglia's little southern beach by swimming, or having been carried by the current.

Alone? What reckless madman would ever have undertaken such a sea journey by himself?

In fearful expectation of the arrival of other, more aggressive shipwrecked companions, quick-thinking men of action decided to reinforce lookouts to the south, from where the danger had appeared timorously for the moment in the imposing but harmless figure of the stranger.

The necessary precautions having first been taken, the Povegliotti conformed to the sacrosanct rule of offering refuge to anyone who had survived death by drowning – the hospitality required of them by the law of the seas: they gave him a bed in the hut outside the village, used for keeping animals during the winter, and in his own way the stranger showed immediate gratitude and a great willingness to adapt.

Before long the stranger constructed a little dwelling for himself, using materials that had been washed ashore, in a part of the island that was completely uninhabited.

He spent his days on the little jetty, trying to lend a hand with the repair of the vessels damaged by the storm and showing a special aptitude for this kind of work: he was familiar with all the techniques of caulking, but it became apparent that his greatest talent was for chopping wood with an axe, to make new planks for the bottom of the boat, and planing to perfection the timber for the oars and the planking. Those big hands with prominent tendons and long thin deft fingers that would stroke the raw wood as if to detect the soul of the material and to follow its secret veins; he wielded the axe like a paintbrush, with short sharp little touches for the initial shaping, then with the plane he removed with assured delicacy the remaining excess – very little in fact – wasting nothing but the bare minimum of wood necessary. In his hands the planking took shape almost naturally.

Then he would gather up the few resulting shavings on the ground and put them in a basket that at the end of the day he would take away with him after exchanging a glance with the head of the boatyard, who would respond with a nod of assent.

He soon won the respect and trust of the wary Povegliotti who nicknamed him Raspa, partly because of his skill with the file and partly because of the abrasive language he spoke that rasped in his mouth.

And when, one day in May, they were short of a sixth rower in the *peota da remurcio* (the flat-bottomed tow-boat), the barrier of islander suspicion completely melted away before Raspa's unspoken offer to take the sick man's place, appearing already at the oar, silent and vaguely smiling, his eyes fixed on those of the stroke in charge of the crew. It immediately became obvious that his was the strongest and most powerful oar in the boat; he was untiring, managing to manoeuvre the blade as if it were the natural extension of his mighty, long, hairy arms.

After that he never missed a single call-out, facing with the same quiet confidence good days, when the Lagoon was like a millpond, and squally days with the Canale dell' Orfano furiously lashed by an east wind, as dangerous as ever.

The mystery of his past never cleared, even after ten years living on the island, of his own free will affably sharing the dangers of the Lagoon and the work on the jetty.

He never talked about himself, using the few words of Venetian dialect that he soon learned, to say at once politely and gruffly only what was necessary in the boat and in the yard. Always very reserved and careful in his manner and in his ways, Raspa was adept at keeping under control a restless nature that occasionally – but only momentarily – revealed itself through the tension in his jaws, which he kept clenched like pincers, and in the sudden darting of his blazing eyes. Basically, he was not so very different from his island hosts who appreciated in him exactly those qualities of contained strength, of being used to hard work, and of discretion, combined with a never failing willingness to help, a hidden gentleness disclosed in those friendly little gestures reserved in particular for his fellow rowers and the children who were always surrounding him, ever since they had seen him one evening, right before their eyes, make a little doll out of wood shavings and fish glue.

Almost every evening afterwards, a small group of youngsters would venture as far as his hut to behold the amazing spectacle of, first, the modelling, then the painting of little figures, a different one every time. In silence, almost in contemplation, they would gather round the stranger, bent over a rudimentary table in the middle of the shack's only room, to watch those long fingers of his deftly working the wood and glue until he had conferred on them the form of a human figure.

They did not realise straightaway that all those little creatures, dressed in little bits of coloured cloth, with jute or threads of dried seaweed for hair, were likenesses of their own people, each with a different expression, each of different build.

This discovery was made by the brightest of the Baffos, Zanetto, son of Jacomo. The evening of new year's day, a windy first of March that did not feel as if spring was yet on its way, as the new figure of a man with a long hooked nose emerged from the skilful hands of the stranger, noticing the little model was missing a right thumb, Zanetto broke the contemplative silence, exclaiming, "Hey, that's my dad!"

No one laughed. The man raised his head, looked him in the eye and, smiling, nodded.

Then they all began to examine with new attentiveness the little figures that over time had come to form a small crowd on the long bench against the wall, like a silent community keeping Raspa company in his isolated hut. That is when they found in each one of them an obvious likeness, to their fathers, mothers, relatives, in short to all the people on the island, men, women, old folk, all standing there staring into space, with their little faces turned towards the stranger, their eyes painted with whiting and lampblack, their smiling mouths marked in the red paint of the *peota da remurchio* – painted red so it could be seen even in storms.

They, the children, were the only ones missing from that silent public, but no one asked Raspa the reason why, imagining perhaps you had to be a grown-up to deserve that honour. The most curious thing was that none of the children betrayed the secret of that discovery, as if by tacit agreement not one of them mentioned at home the wonderful dual existence, in the flesh and in miniature, of their own people.

The stranger vanished, just as he had appeared, one evening in mid February during a storm preceded by a change in the wind direction: no one saw him the morning after the storm, either in the boat yard or on the *remurchio* jetty.

Hoping to find him at home, they approached with discretion – none of the adults had ever been inside the hut – calling out to him, but there was no reply. Then they went to the steward, as he should be the one to enter the hut.

The only light in the windowless room came through the door, so the steward had to leave it wide open in order to be able to see anything.

He needed a few moments before his eyes adapted to the gloom; he felt uncomfortable, as if he were doing something forbidden. Standing on the threshold, he tried to say something – "Where are you? Are you ill?" – that sort of thing, in a low voice; but the words died away in the emptiness, as if absorbed into the void. He could not find the courage to go inside.

Then his eyes began to see.

In the middle of the small room was a table with a stool beside it and a wide bench against the wall with a straw mattress on it – his bed.

There were no belongings anywhere – no clothes, no bowl

or plate by the hearth, no fire burning. Completely empty, as if no one had ever lived in that stark, bare room. But in a recess, hidden by the open door – he realised as he was leaving – a recess that was the full height of the east-facing wall, he saw something and gave a start.

It was him, the stranger, with his arms raised, against the wall, motionless.

An uncontrollable terror overcame the steward – he could not help but flee from that vision, screaming.

Outside the hut was gathered the little delegation of men, the stranger's crewmates and fellow workers at the boat yard, waiting for the outcome of the inspection. They knew Iseppo Ingiostro, the steward, well, the man who took the decisions among them, who assumed the role, not an easy one, of leader of the Poveglia community in the delicate issue, too, of the distribution of income from the *remurchio*; they had seen him fight against the Malamocchini for their sacrosanct rights of towing and fishing, they had heard him negotiate with the Serenissima Signoria, yet never, never had they seen him like this before, beside himself, shocked, terrified.

He tried to say something about Raspa, or rather about his body, transfixed behind the door, with his arms raised, naked, but the words came out confused, stuttered.

Then they all plucked up their courage and went in together, not before having lit a lamp; but they dared not close the door behind them, they closed it just enough so they could see what Iseppo Ingiostro had told them was hidden in a recess beside the door.

Not a sound could be heard, not even the breathing of those dozen big burly men, used to facing the perils of the sea.

Silent, motionless, their eyes wide, they stood in a semi-circle round that wonderful and terrible thing.

The dim light of the lamp allowed them limited vision.

In that tall brick recess stood a very pale body, its raised arms and torso and slightly bent legs – but were they not touching the ground, was he suspended? – forming a Y shape. His chest tensed under the strain of that unnatural position revealed his rib-cage above a hollowed abdomen. A little white cloth draped round his loins was the only garment covering that very fine ivory-white skin.

The person holding the lamp – how the flame trembled! – raised it a little to cast more light on the upper part of the body.

And they saw the face, bowed down, that thin face framed by a beard, with prominent cheekbones. It was his, and not his. Partially covering his temples were long locks of reddish hair falling forward from his head, which had a crown placed on it – a kind of crown.

Slowly the terror that kept them petrified turned into a shared feeling of intense pity and wonder. The details started to become clear, evident: the body's hands and feet were nailed to two planks of wood, one laid across the other behind his shoulders. They had before their eyes a crucified body.

But it was not the stranger, who had been of robust build until yesterday, his skin darker, his face broader, yet there was so much of him in that figure: the hair, the beard of the same tawny colour, of the same length, the tapering hands, legs, feet.

That crucified body was and was not the stranger, but the figure certainly radiated, mysteriously, a tortured familiarity.

The steward – by that stage he had regained his voice and

his usual character – moving closer and thereby casting more light, examined it carefully, seeking some indication, some explanation: the crown was a length of hawser tied around the head and the little cloth round the loins was nothing other than a bit of canvas from an old sail, and the wood used for the cross was two old mooring posts from the pile at the back of the boat yard. He stretched out a hand and touched one of the knees of the body with his index finger: not, it was not flesh, it was not skin, bone, blood, but painted wood.

They all continued to keep silent, paralysed, only the shaking of Iseppo Ingiostro's head stirred the air in that scene of immobility.

Then, retreating – without turning their backs on the body in the recess – they left in silence, closed the door, and first the steward, then all the others, almost furtively, quickly crossed themselves.

No trace of the stranger was to be found anywhere on the island, but when the children began to recount what they had seen him do, telling of his skill in modelling wood shavings with glue, of all the little figures created by his hands, exact, perfect copies of the islanders – which had also disappeared along with their maker – then and only then did they understand that the crucifix was the last and greatest gift of that mysterious man – himself a gift of the sea – left behind to protect these rough, quarrelsome, indomitable, proud and generous folk, the people of Poveglia.

The crucifix, an object of the most fervent devotion among the Povegliotti, is of undocumented origin.

Dating from around the early decades of the fourteenth

century, it probably comes from the Dalmatian coast, since the use of the poor material, papier-mâché, to represent devotional figures belongs to the tradition of Dalmatian sacred art, just as the particular position of the arms forming a Y shape occurs frequently in nordic iconography.

The Christ figure's hair is human, the crown of thorns is actually a length of hawser, the body, made of gesso and stucco, is of extremely great realism and emotional intensity, the modelling is accurate in its detailing of the muscles tensed under strain, in the anatomy of the limbs, in the tortured, gaunt spirituality of the face.

The crucifix was for centuries regarded as miraculous, so much so that the confraternity of the Povegliotti, even after the dispersal of the inhabitants of the island to various parts of the city continued to call their statute of rights and obligations the "Mariegola of the Miraculous Christ of Poveglia and San Vidal our Protector".

With the departure from the island of its pugnacious inhabitants, the crucifix was for a long time kept in the church of San Vitale, until 17 September 1809, when it was solemnly transported on a *peota*, with an escort of six monks, to a monumental altar in the church of Santa Maria dell'Assunzione on Malamocco, where it is to this day an object of pious esteem not far from another statue made of wood – a gift of the sea – representing the Madonna and Child, an object of enthusiastic popular worship: the Madonna di Marina.

A very brief aside regarding this wooden representation of the Mother of Jesus will not take us too far out of the way of our Poveglia tour; on the contrary, it corroborates the strange little story in the pages above, redirecting our gaze a few hundred metres across the short stretch of the Lagoon that lies between Poveglia and Malamocco.

The story goes that one morning, out of a log of wood washed up by the sea and picked up by a resident of Malamocco came an apparition of the Mother of God, crowned and radiant.

As a result of that miraculous apparition, dating back to the fourteenth century, the log made into a statue became the Madonna del Zocco (Madonna of the Log), that every year on the second Sunday of July is carried in procession through the streets of the small centre of Malamocco, after a select group of worshippers, in the church behind locked doors, has seen to the solemn dressing of the statue with pieces from the trousseau assembled over the centuries thanks to donations from the Malamocco faithful.

The Madonna di Marina holds in her arms a wooden effigy of the Baby Jesus, a later addition. Recently a copy of the Madonna del Zocco has been made in order to preserve the original from possible damage during the crowded and impassioned parade, but apparently the ordinary folk of Malamocco have openly demonstrated their bitter objection to this.

Obviously the decision to protect the ancient wooden statue shows wisdom and consideration, given the fragility of this work of fourteenth-century origin: it was probably a ship's figurehead, of oak and limewood, brought to the beaches of Malamocco by the shallow treacherous waters of the Gulf of Venice, that small stretch of sea that unites and divides Istria and the Po River Delta coastline.

So, there they are together, in silent and close communion, beneath the high trusses of the fine parish church of Malamocco, two fascinating testimonies of the mysterious and fruitful familiarity the waters are capable of establishing between places far apart and apparently unrelated to each other. The sea has been and is the planet's greatest peacemaker, the best ambassador for civilisation, in spite of humanity's limited horizons.

Perhaps the ancient inhabitants of Poveglia would not have approved of entrusting their miraculous Christ to the Malamocchini of all people. There was bad blood between the inhabitants of either side of the canal, always inclined to recrimination with regard to fishing rights and towing rights in their shared stretch of water.

And while the heirs of the founders of Metamauco, Padova's port in the Roman era, could claim to have been the earliest citizens of the Lagoon and the not inconsiderable virtue of having "saved" the mortal remains of San Marco from the Infidel, thanks to Buono of Malamocco and Rustico of Torcello (these names provide food for thought!) whose abduction of the relics from Alexandria in Egypt is legendary, the belligerent nature of the unruly and somewhat anarchic Povegliotti found it hard to submit to the rules imposed by the city's administration.

The insufficient submissiveness of the people of Poveglia was the cause of the forced abandonment of the island, as the contentious matter of the War of Chioggia demonstrates – when the Genoese, having set their sights on the bronze horses of San Marco (those horses, *spolia opima* of the treacherous Corsican!), tried to lay siege to the city, getting as far as Malamocco and from there threatening its security.

It was 1378 and the Most Serene Government decided to

evacuate Poveglia, whose inhabitants offered little assurance of trustworthiness, despite the dogal kisses. In fact it was suspected, not completely without justification, that there was a certain goodwill on the part of the Povegliotti towards the Ligurian enemy besieging Chioggia with the support of the Padovan Francesco da Carrara (but were not the Padovans the first inhabitants of the island?).

Given the strategic position of Poveglia, better not to take any risks.

So the senate approved the construction of an octagonal fort overlooking the canal and therefore an extremely sensitive defensive position in the event of the sacred waters of the Lagoon basin being penetrated; on that occasion the population, we can imagine with what enthusiastic acceptance, was moved out (deported) and wisely dispersed among various parishes in San Trovaso, Sant' Agnese and on the Giudecca.

Since then our truculent Poveglia has never regained its former standing: it was a place of quarantine for shipping and an auxiliary isolation hospital during the great outbreaks of plague, when there was not enough space for the plague-ridden in the nearby Lazzaretto Vecchio, or in the Lazzaretto Nuovo, built on the island opposite Sant'Erasmo. There is a fascinating but unsubstantiated theory that Zorzi da Castelfranco – Giorgione – whose life is still deeply shrouded in mystery, actually ended up on Poveglia during the plague of 1510, having contracted the disease, it is said, from his lover, and there his bones lay, now dissolved by the salty earth.

After its proud inhabitants had been dispersed, it was as if the soil of that world were showing itself to be secretly hostile to other people and other uses; the Magistracy of Old

Public Accounts in 1527 had offered the little island to the Camaldolese order, a plan that was never realised. But not even the descendants of ancient Povegliotti lineage, scattered round the city, accepted the invitation of the Magistracy to return to the home of their forefathers to rebuild a community.

Towards the end of the seventeenth century and also of the Republic's existence, the island was taken over by the Magistracy of Public Health. It was later a shipyard, using the *tezon grande* (large warehouse) – already built for health purposes (for quarantined goods), of the kind that existed on every quarantine island in the Lagoon – as a depot for repair materials for ships needing work on their hulls. Later and until the middle of the last century it was used as a maritime health station, whose buildings, today rather ghostly on the waterfront overlooking the canal that separates the octagon from the rest of the island, incorporated the bell tower, used as a lighthouse.

Despite initiatives taken by the San Marco government to repopulate Poveglia with monks and nuns, potential inhabitants of a more peaceable nature, no convent or spiritual retreat was ever established here, nor any other form of religious community.

Perhaps because of its history of independence and secularity, or more likely because it was for a long time a place of confinement for plague victims and more recently for the mentally ill, the island has entered the popular imagination as an accursed place, where the spirits of the damned roam, something that even today attracts the would-be ghostbuster to its inhospitable shores. Every summer local newspapers have yet another entertaining anecdote to report about ill-prepared hunters of lost souls who themselves get lost, on nights when there is a full moon, in this densely overgrown patch of earth crowded with spectral shadows.

There are those who say that sinister sounds, like wailing, emanate from the island, but as we know, fancy is the best nutrient for the soil of abandoned places.

However, the earth of that uncultivated island, having once belonged to an indomitable people, has given rise to a strength of resistance, a will for independent life, almost as if the traces of a small rebellious population had germinated in the rugged, fecund soil of Poveglia, imparting to the overgrown brambles and the few scrawny cherry trees left behind by hopeful gardeners of the past an exceptional vigour that encourages leaves, flowers and fruit to overlay each other in abundance, offering the spectacle of rare, almost monstrous, fertility.

We like to imagine there is an atmosphere imbued with bellicose energy lingering above this little patch of land, an invincible inclination of the genius loci to distance itself from the governing power, true to this home of anarchic spirits, a proudly, irredeemably secular snippet of Lagoon history, a no-man's land, therefore belonging to all, in the salty bowel of the kindly southern Lagoon.

LIDO

Altino and Concordia.

Anyone who lived in Venice before the great exodus that began in the middle of the 1970s, these names do not correspond solely and primarily to two ancient cities of the Veneti on the shores of the north Lagoon; for those who lived through the excited expectation in the early days of June – when spring had not yet officially given way to summer – of the return of the great Lido "season", those two names evoke heat, the promise of joy, liberty.

The start of the season of marine pleasures coincided for the families of local citizens with the end of the school year: then the City would empty of youngsters and children, daily transported in compact masses packed onto the legendary ferries *Altino* and *Concordia* that departed regularly three times an hour (at 7-27-47, on the dot) from the main boat landing at Ponte della Paglia to make the short happy journey to the Santa Maria Elisabetta dock on the Lido.

Those ferry crossings were an integral part of the marine day: crowded on the departure landing, we readied ourselves for it, starting to push, trying to get to the front, as soon as the ferry came into sight, that is to say well before it was halfway on its journey towards us. We were crushed together, hot, yelling, jostling, the older ones clutching lilos, the younger ones buckets and spades, confident of an imminent delight: the freshness on the top deck of the above-mentioned *Concordia* and/or *Altino*, while deep discussions went on, all centred on the collective organisation of the day on the beach under the banner of alliances that were no less unstable than unreliable.

Memorable journeys, real free-booting assaults to grab seats – of which there were many but not an unlimited number – on the upper deck of the big boat (those happy days when big cruise ships were still a long way off) that into the bargain had the exquisite delight of a little bar to offer, sweaty sticky Buondi Motta cakes and melting chocolate bars of Ciocori.

Inevitably, those who had not managed to find room above, not even standing, not even squeezed six together on a bench, not even sitting astride the giant square-shaped lifebelts piled up in the stern, resigned themselves: in despair and disarray the rest of what was one of the most vociferous groups of children went back down the stairs they had climbed with proud self-confidence to find somewhere to sit not on the lower deck of the ferry – reserved for mothers and babies in pushchairs – but in the deeper recesses of the boat, the room in the bow, partly below the waterline, ill lit, smelling of fuel oil and deafening, with the raspy roar of the diesel coming from the engine room – a veritable mouth of hell, a den where invisible men lurked.

There were some who deliberately chose to go "below", but this would usually be on the return journey, coming back after a day on the beach, towards sunset; the little enclave generally suited a variable number of child couples, whose relationships, like tender and fragile inflorescences sensitive to sunrays, had blossomed on the baking-hot sand during the day at the seaside. Taking advantage of the limited appeal of the seats in the lower depths, they sought and found brief but sufficient privacy to swear eternal love to each other and to exchange sticky and embarrassed demonstrations of affection on salty, sandy skin reddened by ultraviolet rays and by passion just as innocent as adolescents can be.

But the *Concordia/Altino* is now docking, the creaking rope secured by the crewman's expert throw of the line over the big bollard on the boat landing, and the throngs of inflatable plastic, with the best of Venice's youth trudging behind, disperse across the sunny square, beneath the benevolent and welcoming CAMPARI sign that towers over it, a square that is a bridgehead of temptations, where modernity and the lures of the mainland await – because the Lido's island nature is barely recognised by the aquatic spirits of true-born Venetians.

There on that same cobbled square, looking towards the very faint broken lines of the City's re-emerging profile – already vaguely dissolving in the promise, always borne out, of the heat haze that like a loving mother envelops the Lagoon Queen every summer's day – was substantiation of the fruitful and ancient dichotomy in the spirit of the citizenry between commoner and aristocrat, compelled of necessity to co-exist in the straitened geographies of stone and water and at last free to reveal itself in the distribution of themselves along the shores of the Lido according to a rigid social distinction.

Those, in fact, who set off on foot, trudging over the porphyry cobblestones of the broad pavements of the Gran Viale – offering real temptations to spend money, with the new Standa (a chain of supermarkets, at that time a symbol of modernity) on the left and the joys, forbidden to the most hard-up, of the Parco delle Rose phantasmagorical dodgem cars – make their way eastwards, to the so-called Zone A public beach, with poor facilities but gloriously free. The remainder, no sooner released from the capacious and democratic bowels of the *Concordia/Altino*, crowd as densely as the impenetrability of bodies will allow into the even-to-this-day lamented trolley-bus of the ACNIL (Azienda Comunale di Navigazione Interna Lagunare, which ran Venice's public transport system 1930-78) – also identified with an A, perhaps in an attempt to mislead or perhaps for lack of imagination – that jauntily heads for the "smarter" beaches: Des Bains, Consorzio, Quattro Fontane, Excelsior, before making its way down – the Lido is topographically flat, so down is used in a metaphoric sense – towards the far west of the Civil Servants' and the Sorriso seaside establishments, coming to the end of the line at the sweet-smelling Riding Club, on the Lagoon side, opposite the island of Lazzaretto Vecchio.

The trolley-bus is the most trying part of the journey for the aspiring bathers but by now the end is within sight, with the unfolding spectacle from the clear windows (always sealed shut for security reasons incomprehensible to any human being) of the much yearned-for restless blue lying behind the splendid curtain of maritime pines lining the seashore on the left.

And straight away it is clothes off and ghastly high-protection sunscreen lavishly slapped on by loving parental hands even on cloudy days.

Days at once endless and very short, gloriously filled with aquatic inventions, frenetic sessions of tamburello and rackets at the water's edge, furious marble contests on a roughly constructed playing area in the sand, illicit "volcanoes" – but only at dusk when the lifeguards are less vigilant – and sandcastles with internal passageways with little lighted beacons inside them. Football totally prohibited, on pain of irrevocable confiscation of the ball by the white-coated beach wardens. But above all, absolute top of the list of seaside activities, is the dangerous game of "tag", among the cement ruins of the little jetty, at the end of which, awaiting never-to-be-realised restoration, a reinforced concrete grille looks out over the sea with its square eyes: there is the greatest real danger of slipping and banging one's little head (by definition, thoughtless) on the protruding girders, then of falling into the water and – perhaps – dying.

Endless days, never long enough for the children, who generally established themselves on the shoreline in front of the family beach hut (*"capanna"* as the locals call it), more or less within sight of mother and always within earshot for the frequent snack breaks that provided sufficient energy to carry on with more reinvented seaside games.

The pattern of the day was almost exactly the same

all along the beach, but the caste distinctions between the different beach concessions were rigorously reflected not only in the beach hut furnishings – soft cushions and striped towelling covers on teak chaise-longues at Des Bains and the Excelsior, ordinary canvas deckchairs at the others – but also and especially in their toilet and shower facilities.

In June 1967 – many remember it as the beginning of a new epoch – came the signs of Rebirth after the terrible November of 1966, which had literally devastated, as well as the City, so much of the Venetian estuary, including the Lido. Having shaken off the homely atmosphere of the 1950s and the unsophisticated luxuries of boom-time Italy, the beaches of the Moorish-style grand hotel and the unforgettable hotel of Aschenbach were radically updated, offering the never-satisfied habitués of the latest creature-comforts the unimaginable pleasure of hot water showers in sparkling tiled bathrooms, together with a new look for the beach huts of obsolete plywood panels and tin roofs, replaced, at the Excelsior, with white Arab-style tents that each had a big smoked glass ball on top, and at Des Bains, with straw-roofed wooden huts. An allusion to our Bel Paese's colonial past? An opening-up to "other" cultures, a demonstration of interracial ecumenism?

But this development was fraught with unsuspected consequences.

It was precisely at this point of greatest distinction that there was evidence for the first time of beach caste laws being infringed, of irreversible contamination.

Initially, with diffidence and subdued discretion, in ones and twos, but very soon without restraint, in big noisy groups, they came from the other beaches – even from Zone A, it is reported – young bathers with bottles of Badedas and egg/zabaione-scented shampoos to enjoy illicitly the unbelievable luxury of the hot showers within the exclusive confines of the Excelsior/Des Bains.

To no avail were the measures promptly taken by the CIGA administration – which ran the grand hotels standing behind the beaches – to deal with the phenomenon: despite doubling the number of staff on duty, and urging the already stern inspectors in their dazzling uniforms to be even tougher, the infiltration from the bathing world beyond the pale did not end. Raucousness, shower foams, the progressive clogging up with sand of the precious teak decking on the bathroom floors, exuberant joking and fooling around, the demolition of the male/female dividers – this degradation intruded among the fragrant beds of pittosporum, oleander and star jasmine of the luxury resort, and nothing was as before.

Beleaguered in body and soul, the habitués of seaside comfort, after repeated protests – no less forceful than vain – addressed to the beach hut offices, resigned themselves to seeing the erosion, season by season, of their marine paradise, so discriminatingly arrived at thanks to the super exclusive CIGA motorboat service, whose gleaming vessels transported them from the waterfront of the Gritti and Danieli hotels to the Excelsior dock.

Little by little, that dreadful iniquity of democratic bathing spread from the hot showers even to the Diga Grande rotonda, all decked with flags of rearing colts, and spilled over onto the – alas for them! – state-owned water's edge.

And the luxury-brand Lido, the Grande Lido of the golden

age, the Lido of Thomas Mann and the stars of cinema began its unstoppable decline.

The Lido "season" is a thing of the past, the City's marine *paradeisos* consigned to memory and to family photo albums.
Something quite different lay ahead.
The Lido of today, in these depressing times, is the result of the combined efforts of political operators and economic conjurers: the building speculation of the '70s and '80s; the neglect and (closing down) sale of the very fine hospital unit on the Lido; the cutting down of the historic pine wood in front of the Casino to make way for a white elephant, creating an economic black hole that has cost taxpayers 40 million euros; the despoliation, closure and neglect of the Hotel des Bains; the long list of horrors – and towering above all in terms of cost, riskiness, and impact, the MOSE project – perpetrated in this narrow strip of earth and sand that closes off the Lagoon from the sea has battered and buffeted the lovely back drop to the San Marco basin.
And yet, in its cool streets named after the giants of La Serenissima, among the yellow-lichen-covered stones of one of the most suggestive cemeteries in the world – the beautiful old Jewish cemetery, among the maritime pines of the San Nicolò/*Sanicoleto* pine wood – over the dunes of Alberoni with their dense growth of pioneer vegetation, on the Murazzi's doughty blocks of sun-baked Istrian stone, among the bunkers camouflaged with thick brambles (Lido blackberries have an unparalleled flavour of the sea, a perfect balance of saltiness and wild-berry sweetness), still persisting, clinging to memory, to the light, to the magic of that briny smell

mingled with tamarisk and marram grass, to the changing and ever regenerative mood of the pale Adriatic of the north, is a diffidently wild beauty, a breath of simple life yet possible, an air of the elemental and the marginal, an enduring security perimeter, no-man's-land, Lagoon border.

SAN GIORGIO IN ALGA

The little island that floats like a piece of crumpled confetti at the junction of the Canale di Fusina and the Canale di Contorta Sant'Angelo della Polvere early on got the name by which it is called today: San Giorgio in Alga.

The name derives from a chapel dedicated in the thirteenth century to the dragon-slaying saint by the Gatilesa or Gattara family, and as for that natural ornament, the algae, under pressure of the converging currents from the old mouth of the Brenta, not very far away at that time, seaweed gathered in abundance in that part of the western Lagoon, today dominated by the controversial and in its own way fascinating skyline indented with the chimneys and arches of the Marghera oil refinery.

Filling the lower horizon, those lines that now appear familiar to us – and almost beautiful when observed from the opposite shore of our beloved salt-water basin, from the Lido or San Pietro in Volta or Pellestrina – reflect metallic gleams not too dissimilar from those on the sharp pinnacles of the City's bell towers and on the matronly roundedness of its cupolas, which Brodsky imagined as teapots, in the soft interludes of light when it is not yet dawn or no longer dusk; and the rays, or rather the precursors or followers of rays in the form of luminous scorch marks, catch the heights of that man-made landscape in just the same way. Further away, the western backdrop to the Lagoon stage, are the little dark teeth of the Euganean Hills, extinct volcanos in a rhythmic sequence. It would be a bold outsider who admitted to seeing any beauty in the Marghera skyline: artificial and extraneous, these places of work and contamination seem materialisations from other worlds, from another history that has nothing to do with the Lagoon's past; yet to the eye of a native-born Venetian, in accordance with that strange paradox, which nevertheless always holds true, whereby what is familiar is instilled with a special beauty – those jagged lines, the lance-like chimneys, the jib arms of the cranes, the broad metallic arches of the pipelines are irreversibly part of the mental landscape, constituent elements of an *inscape* now just as authentic as the mother tongue.

But if we look back to the City's era of paradise, when the water not the land was supreme, when the water not the land determined the rhythm of the seasons and imposed awareness of mankind's total dependency on its changeable nature – with its rages as well as its complaisancies – during that long period of union when the Lagoon was the vast nuptial bed of an ever-renewed pact based on respect, we can still decipher geographies capable of striking a perfect balance.

So let us imagine small boats made of reeds, little more than a raft, and men of the land who leave places that have become hostile, unsafe, seeking to make a life among the resources of those treacherous, as yet unknown waters.

Let us imagine the ever greater distance between the shore and the low horizon, with its refracted deceptive light: long oar-strokes cutting through the rippling surface, the quiet sound of that gesture amid the silence that follows the awakening of the marsh birds, the water prairie surrounding the craft – so fragile, so alien. The man probes the depths with his eyes, trying to distinguish the variations of colour that signal changes in the currents: he fears danger but is looking for food and moving ever further away from the mainland, now invisible, behind him. Then slowly, at the edge of visibility, a dark form materialises, a larger ripple, a broad shadow in the water: the man strives to keep faith, he does not recognise in that apparition the shore he has left behind, but he senses that what he sees in the distance is land suspended in the water, and as he gradually draws nearer, he begins to distinguish treetops, dense vegetation.

He does not yet know what an island is.

He seeks an approach among the sandy shallows, gets out of his boat with the water coming up to his shoulders, drags the boat along, sinking at every step into the mud that sucks at his feet, and a field of seaweed closes in around his body.

It is a grassy water, thick and smelly, streaked with browns and reds.

He moves forward, opening up a passage through that yielding, caressing stuff with his chest. He secures the little boat above the narrow beach of grey sand, and starts to make his way through the vegetation, cautiously.

Our man's adventure is his discovery of the island, the wonder and fear inspired by a different kind of place, like land but surrounded by sea; it has constrictive boundaries but infinite horizons, it is a safe refuge yet a vulnerable haven, at the mercy of the natural elements: he is a man alone in a wilderness of water. Everything that happens will depend on this liquid element, fresh water and salt water: the possibility of survival, the establishment of a community, the development of a micro economy, expansion.

The fate of man condensed in a scrap of land.

Island and isolation: the desire to live in harmony with the other, and the instinct to dominate; security within borders and the need for new conquests. The island is the objective correlative of human nature, and maybe of love.

This is how I like to think of the fate of that island, San Giorgio in Alga, and of the first man to enter that little aquatic universe: he came upon it, tamed it, erected a tiny church to invoke the gods, to sanctify the bond, he ennobled it and made it different from his own nature, he summoned others to enjoy it because his were the merit and the glory – so it pleased the gods – and then he abandoned it, leaving it in the state we see it in today, wrecked, ruined, stripped of every asset, deserted even by the seaweed that no longer encircles it, having been replaced by the phantasmagoria of materials and colours constituted by the detritus of so-called civilisation.

But if the fate of San Zorzi in Alega (in the Venetian spelling) is what we have before our eyes today, while sadly navigating the Canale di Contorta Sant' Angelo with the apocalyptic prospect of an ominous new assault on the Lagoon bed to facilitate the access of floating monsters, the august and centuries-long past of the first little island that presented itself to whoever came into the Lagoon from the west, allows us to make another brief and not completely fanciful exploration of the place, with the help of a little imagination, and some historical documents and magnificent engravings, in particular the two views of the island, of 1696, by Padre Vincenzo Coronelli, the great cartographer of La Serenissima.

At the time of the geographer monk, the small island of San Zorzi in Alega had a solid reputation as a place of hospitality, capable of offering even a sumptuous reception to illustrious guests.

It was precisely its position to the far west of the City, lying on the Lizza Fusina-Bacino di San Marco route via the Giudecca Canal, that made it a Lagoon "gateway" for pilgrims and ambassadors coming from the mainland on a visit to La Serenissima (just as the island of San Secondo was for those coming from the north), aided in this role by an architectural structure that had been enriched over the centuries, probably from the fourteenth century onwards, given that as early as 1328 the island was the selected location for hosting the celebration of the marriage between Mastino della Scala and Taddea dei Carrara, and the related festivities.

The presence, between 1400 and the fall of the Republic, of various monastic orders, from the Benedictines, to the

Augustinians and even the Barefoot Carmelites, affords us an image of San Zorzi in Alega as an island characterised by a spiritual uncertainty, land suspended between sky and water, a retreat favouring meditation and prayer, a refuge of inspired souls intolerant of worldly pomp and clamour.

Such was the case for two young priests of noble family, Antonio Correr and Gabriele Condulmer. These two aristocrats, scorning those worldly things that would have been theirs by right of ancestry, founded a small community of seventeen young men – the "commune" of today – inspired by the "harsh and pure" preaching of Giovanni Dominici, a true conqueror of souls who – at a time when, and in a State where, religion was considered ancillary to politics – managed to win respect and attention from the highest authorities of the Signoria, even to the extent of influencing their opinions and decisions.

It is said that the cells of the Corpus Christi convent could not contain all the young women fired with a monastic vocation ignited in those innocent little heads by the impassioned words of Dominici. The preacher's influence, which it seems was the driving force behind the temporary expulsion of the Jews from the City in 1397, upset a great many people, so much so that there were as many as seven attempts made on his life, but seven times did fate, or heavenly protection, spare him.

But the ways of the world and its intrigues did not find fertile soil in the souls of the seventeen young men who preferred to go into retreat in San Nicolò del Lido during those difficult times when Venice was at war with the Genoese. It was because of the extremely delicate strategic position of the monastery on the Lido that our community of young seminarists was soon relocated to San Zorzi in Alega, under the benevolent protection of Ludovico Barbo, prior on the island, and there it grew in virtue and merit, with the two young patricians later becoming, Antonio, a cardinal and, Gabriele, even Pope, under the name of Eugenio IV, and as if that were not enough, with the same tiny community, abounding in celestial inspiration, even producing a saint: Lorenzo Giustiniani, who rose through the ecclesiastical hierarchy, becoming first Bishop of Castello, then Patriarch.

Indeed it was Lorenzo Giustiniani who transformed that small group of young men into a proper religious congregation, of which he became prior, extending its relations – today we would say "networking" – with other monasteries. The small community of seventeen established for themselves a way of life inspired by poverty, sharing and prayer, at the same time allowing its lay participants the freedom not to take vows.

The little congregation adopted rules and wore a sky-blue (*celeste* in Italian) habit, perhaps to underline a special relationship with Heaven, or perhaps because it was the dominant colour of the horizon from the island, or more likely because it was the cheapest material available. From their distinctive habit, which spread well beyond the confines of the Lagoon, reaching as far as Portugal, the congregation took the name of Celestines.

The island, it was said, had a representational role in the sophisticated liturgy of the Republic's reception of visitors: nothing was left to chance on the occasions when the standard of San Marco was required to make a show of the City's power, so the "location" of the first greeting was continually enriched with symbols worthy of the Lion's economic, military and cultural dominance.

VENICE NOIR

The greatest artistic talents, who, during the extraordinary period of sixteenth-century Venetian painting were teaching the world the use of colour, were summoned to make the island magnificent. Works by the marvellous Muranese artists Antonio and Bartolomeo Vivarini were brought together on San Zorzi in Alega, along with a splendid "Nativity" by Cima da Conegliano, even Giovanni Bellini had a commission from the island, while the church's altarpiece came from Veronese's workshop. All gathered in serene triumph of beauty beneath the high roof of the church of San Giorgio with its austere Romanesque facade, just as it appears in Coronelli's view; and we imagine it with a sober and soaring interior, a single nave lit by two large Diocletian windows in the long side walls, all focusing on the apse with its blind arches, a connecting element with the most secluded and private part of the island, the monastery with its long wing housing the cells, all facing eastwards over the Lagoon.

And if we were to superimpose the delightful view in a late eighteenth-century engraving – crowded with boats and bustling with life in the space on the water in front of the landing on the island – on the wretched image of today, we would still be able clearly to decipher the initial visual impact on visitors who arrived on San Zorzi: the big black mouth of the *cavana*, open to newcomers and resonant with backwash, deep and vaguely menacing like a sea cave, and a few mètres beyond, towards the church parvis, the two slender arches of the entrance to the area assigned for the accommodation of pilgrims, the guesthouse. In the far corner of the gardens, under its pyramidal roof, the small squat tower of the powder magazine – a fundamental necessity for every island after the devastating explosion at the Arsenale in 1569 – behind which can be glimpsed the fine line of the horizon, and rising above it the cupolas of the Redentore and the Zitelle on the Giudecca. Set further back, immersed in the herb garden, a tall building can be discerned that extends into the verdure, perhaps the big library, founded by San Lorenzo Giustiniani, which until the tragic fire in the eighteenth century, contained an exceptional collection of books (including the famous Bible, valued at 60 gold zecchini, a genuine fortune).

Presenting a discreet gracefulness and, for the cornice dentils, the simple elegance of the white stone that came from Istria, with no concession to excess, that is how San Zorzi, as a place of meditation and prayer, must have appeared to the visitor. However the names of the artistic geniuses who operated there would suggest to our imaginations the dazzling power of Venetian art.

But art comes to the aid of our imaginative capabilities, offering us, in the unexpected context of a dramatic crucifixion scene, a full view of the entire complex of San Zorzi. Attributed to the Bergamasco painter Alvise Donato, a canvas of vast dimensions, once located on the island, and now to be found in the Sala Capitolare of the Scuola di San Marco, depicts the crucifixion of Christ in a curious tripartite setting, dense with politico-religious meaning. Landsknecht soldiers mingled with others in Turkish clothing are pictured in the scene at the foot of the three crosses: on the left, against a background of hills and fortresses, flies a Roman vexillum with the traditional Roman emblems and with the three crowns of the Turkish Empire, while on the right appears the two-headed eagle, symbol of the Hapsburgs, allies at that time of the Ottomans.

In the centre, like a pearl in an exquisite niche amid the verdant landscape is the resplendent white convent complex of San Giorgio in Alga, looking out over the calm waters of the Lagoon, complete with gondola. This incongruous view testifies to the geopolitical tensions in the Mediterranean in the sixteenth century, and the delicate position of the Republic, threatened on either side by the two great powers. The islet of San Zorzi placed in the centre of the scene behind Christ's cross, becomes a symbol of La Serenissima, Defender of the Faith, and haven of peace.

A quiet beauty, ideally suited to offering a most serene welcome to pilgrims and royalty, as in 1574, when Henri III visited Venice.

But like everything that appears fresh and pure at birth and after winning success deteriorates and fall into decline, *"...like all earthly things, the zeal in those religious orders cooled"* – wrote Ermolao Paoletti – matching the fate of the City whose rigour of earlier days was now a thing of the past, the Celestine community born on San Zorzi in Alega, over time, allowed itself to be corrupted by the temptations of the world, until they abandoned not only their rule but also the original colour of their tunic to adopt a more luxurious white habit. It was certainly not just because of a colour deviation that towards the mid seventeenth century, after various reprimands and attempts to return the order to a more austere way of life, the congregation was dissolved by order of Pope Clement IX, and the ever prudent government of La Serenissima took advantage of the occasion to use the not inconsiderable assets of the dissolved congregation in the costly, damaging, endless war against the Turks, a continuous financial drain met with ever greater difficulty from the coffers and with ever decreasing confidence of the San Marco gonfalon.

Not long before, a curious event had taken place in the troubled waters of the Lagoon lying before San Zorzi, perhaps a sign of warning against the disintegrating standards of behaviour on our little island; it was the year 1657, Filiasi noted: *"Although the sky was clear, I saw in the lagoon to the west, near San Giorgio in Alga, a white cloud of strange magnitude"* – and thus far, nothing out of the ordinary, the *garbin*, that is, the *libeccio*, the wind lowing from the southwest, is known to bring sudden violent squalls to a Lagoon that looks as flat as a millpond. But, growing bigger, this cloud *"sent a whirlwind towards Venice, that destroyed monasteries, houses and bell towers. A terrible boom was heard and in the end a reddish light appeared in the air and there was a rumble like that (the Chronicles say) from the mouth of a volcano."* The really strange thing was the reaction of the Serenissimo government and its navy, always vigilant against any possible attack from the sea and from the sky, because, *"The vessels fired many cannon shots against the whirlwind, as it passed over the canal leading to the port, having traversed the city. The whole of Venice was in confusion, and it was said* – and this is the significant bit – *that the terrible cloud rose from the depths of the lagoon itself close to San Giorgio in Alga."* Like an immense bubble fuelled by vapours and gases, expanding, and overturning to inflict implacable punishment especially on monasteries and churches. A volcanic bubble of anticlericalism or a foretaste of what would happen some three hundred years later (as we shall see below)?

But as misfortunes never come singly, it so happened,

as in other small jewels of the Lagoon archipelago, that a tremendous fire in the summer of 1716 devastated it beyond retrieval, dispelling in the Lagoon's torpid air its entire artistic and bibliographic heritage.

It was rebuilt and made worthy of receiving so illustrious a visit as that of Pope Pius VI who arrived from Lizza Fusina on the island where Doge Paolo Renier awaited him with a great retinue of clergy and diplomatic representatives.

That was in the year 1782, the same year in which the "Conti del Nord", as they called themselves – that is the future tsar Paul I and his consort – came to the Lagoon. It seems worth mentioning this, because the treatment reserved for these illustrious guests, although of equal rank, was quite different from the arrangements made for the Pope.

For Pavel Petrovich and Maria Feodorovna, La Serenissima displayed all the expertise, luxury and imagination that had made the eighteenth-century City, in its diplomatic tradition and its special attitude to pleasure, an imitable model for the world: the unbridled and, alas, fatal Venetian *joie de vivre* prepared triumphal arches, regattas, processions, banquets, allegorical games, and much more. Obviously the setting for these grandiose celebrations could be no other place than Piazza San Marco, in all its dazzling theatricality and expanse.

By contrast, even allowing for the tone of "sobriety" befitting festivities for a pope, the reception the Serenissima arranged for the papal visit was strategically decentralised to San Giovanni e Paolo. Admittedly, a large vertical platform structure – with very steep steps – was erected on the parvis in front of San Zanipolo; out of all proportion and barely accessible (as Gabriel Bella's canvas shows in great detail), but the Campo – as was well known – could only accommodate a limited crowd of onlookers, despite the temporary planking partially covering the Canale dei Mendicanti. The report on the papal journey, penned by a prelate in the Pope's retinue, is at pains to point out that the installation of the tall and precarious loggia structure in front of the Scuola Grande di San Marco was for the convenience of the Pope, who was staying as a guest in the Dominican monastery, but other less diplomatic versions suggest, however, that it was a deliberate ploy on the part of the Signoria – always distinctly secular and opposed to any personality cult – to keep the event away from the political heart of the City: not in front of the Basilica, but in front of that other but less illustrious, almost second-rate "San Marco", already cunningly used centuries ago to honour the agreement made with Colleoni to erect a memorial to him "in front of San Marco". A clever trick.

Nor did the relationship between Pio VI and Venice end with that visit: as we know, poor Pio VI was to see Rome occupied by the Bonapartists, and himself deposed, taken prisoner and deported to Valence, where he died in 1798; and as it happened, Venice was chosen as the location for the conclave to elect his successor. In a City already gloomily subject to the rule of the Austrian Empire, a very long and very ill-attended conclave, held in the monastery on another island of San Giorgio, not in Alga but Maggiore, after much interference and political intrigue elected Pius VII to the papacy, the very same who would later be forced – *obtorto collo* – to place the Caesarean crown on the clever head of Bonaparte.

But we left our little island of San Zorzi in Alega, a place of comforting and kindly hospitality, shortly after the clamour of the papal visit – with that great procession of boats, among them many a *peaton* (large ceremonial boat) bedecked with crimson velvet so heavy it had to be towed, and welcome salutes fired from the banks of the Giudecca Canal – had all died down, and now, even while the few cardinals are gathered on San Giorgio Maggiore, awaiting the correct inspiration from Heaven and from the Empire, the suffocating cloak of Imperial rule is cast over that blessed little isle of San Zorzi with its algae, transforming the spiritual retreat into a political prison.

It was 1799 when the marchese Azzo Giacinto Malaspina, a Tuscan anticlerical and Bonapartist, was imprisoned, among others, in the deserted cells of the monastery converted for this purpose. And it is a sad story steeped in mystery that surrounds the marchese Malaspina, who ended up on our little island after being moved from prison to prison, in Florence, Mantua and then Venice, and from there to the dark and secure Bay of Kator, before returning to the Lagoon.

We know what he looked like from a physical description of him that the Austrian political police released after the marchese's supposed escape from the island: *Marchese Giacinto Malaspina has escaped from gaol in Venice, where he was held as a prisoner of state; aged 54, 5 feet 10 inches in height, of slim build, with a long face of olive complexion, a long aquiline nose, dark eyes, thick eyebrows and white hair (though not completely white), he was wearing a green coat, grey trousers, a round hat, shoes, and a pigtail: he speaks French well and a little German.*

From this detailed identikit we get the image of a man, although thin and marked by captivity, of proud and noble appearance, elegant, with a big strong nose and deep eyes, lord of the tiny marquisate of Mulazzo, in Lunigiana.

A free spirit, a Jacobin who had taken to heart the revolutionary message and applied it in his little fiefdom, regardless of kith and kin, raising the French tricolour on top of the tower in his citadel on the arrival of the Napoleonic army. We can well understand that such an attitude must have been unacceptable to any form of autocratic power and least of all the Austrians, who laid hands on the liberal marchese as soon as possible, forcing him to go on a penitentiary pilgrimage, doing the rounds of the prisons of the Empire, and indeed ending up at San Giorgio in Alga.

What happened to Azzo Giacinto would seem to be a common story of political imprisonment, concluding with an escape, one of the many sad persecutions of educated and forward-looking minds.

However, events are tinged with mystery, in shades of red and black; this is the tragic fate of a freethinker caught up in the unfolding of History, an intrigue of passion and politics.

Years after the disappearance reported by the Imperial police, artillery lieutenant Teodoro Psalidi, stationed in Verona, who was with Azzo in prison, remembered clearly the writing on the wall of Malaspina's cell, words difficult to decipher, scratched into the plaster by Azzo, who was probably aware of the fate that awaited him. The first line of the graffito was illegible, but the second, a hendecasyllable, read as follows: "A victim of British jealousy, am I."

The background to this dates from the years the marchese

spent at the court of his friend and companion the Grand Duke Leopold of Tuscany. At that time the noble Malaspina had been an assiduously passionate admirer of the beautiful and fiery Alessandra Cini di Montevarchi, married to the dragoon officer Lorenzo Mari, but already a subject of gossip because of her very loose behaviour, a woman actively engaged in civic life, unwilling to bow to the prevailing moral code.

We do not know if and how the relationship between Azzo and Alessandra ended, when the impassioned anti-Bonapartist "Sandrina", as she was known in the Arezzo, was developing a strong political presence, distinguishing herself with her fighting spirit.

What is certain is that, feared and respected in the Viva Maria movement (the Tuscan resistance to the French invasion), Sandrina fought on horseback, leading the ranks of insurgents. At her side, and madly in love with her, according to contemporary reports, was Lord Wyndham, the English envoy to Tuscany and minister plenipotentiary in the organisation of anti-Napoleonic resistance; no doubt quite jealous of the indomitable Sandrina's past, and possibly her present, the Englishman diplomat was well placed to play an instrumental role in the persecution and subsequent capture of the Marchese Malaspina.

Of the supposed escape from San Zorzi in Alega, his prison companion Psalidi gave a very different version from that disclosed by the Austrian commander in the Lagoon, affirming that Azzo did not in fact escape, having been assassinated while in prison on the island, and that the escape was completely staged, with ropes tied to the forced iron bars on the window of the cell to silence any later recrimination regarding the disappearance of the poor marchese. Even today what actually happened remains a mystery, all traces buried in the depths of history.

A few years later the role of accommodating compulsory "guests", a sad epilogue to its illustrious past, also ceased, and the umpteenth Austrian fortress was built on the deserted island.

But twentieth century history adds a brief footnote to the small island's vocation for hospitality: during the Second World War, the steamship *Tampico* was scuttled on the narrow beach of San Giorgio in Alga; an Italian Royal Navy tanker, it was launched in 1908, under a British flag, in a shipyard in Newcastle-on-Tyne, under the name of the *SS Carpathian*.

Put out of commission by repeated attacks during an Italian mission to collect fuel from the Black Sea, it was towed from Piraeus to Venice, to the quiet waters in front of San Zorzi: with its prow embedded in the sand and the floating stern camouflaged, the old tanker, which had navigated deeper waters and more heroic times, became an easy training target for the Gamma men of the 10th Assault Vehicle Flotilla (Decima Flottiglia Motoscafi Armati Siluranti, or X MAS), the combat swimmers and frogmen who found among the remains of the Dominican monastery the ideal conditions for practising their underwater limpet-mine laying.

SAN CLEMENTE

The only days of calm for Maria were those of thick fog, *caligo*, when an impenetrable white curtain fell over the Lagoon and nothing could be seen any more, not even the shores of the island, a few yards from the big white wall of the institute.

All was finally swallowed up, geography and memory disappeared out of sight and out of mind, leaving her vacant, breathing in that micronised suspension of water, sky and sea.

The sluggish salty air that lay stagnant on the Santo Spirito canal reached her like medicine she had been waiting for, yearning for. All smells were lost in it, absorbed as if by a big foamy sponge, it had the colour of absence and like absence succeeded in deadening her dull ache, which too often turned into furious bouts of pain.

She breathed deeply, and the freezing dampness travelled straight as an arrow from her dilated nostrils, reaching that obscure part of her brain that no medication had ever really treated before. She rested her high rounded forehead, like the lid of a white lacquer jewellery box, on the rusty bars over the window, awaiting the certain effect of inhaling the medicinal fog.

It was always like this; after ten years in this place, she was all too familiar with the reaction mechanisms of her distress: it took a few minutes of deep breaths, eventually becoming even and innocuous, of staring into the white blankness, to forget this closed-in horizon crowded with ghosts, each individually recognised, that gnawed away inside her every minute of every day since they had taken her away from her mother's house.

She remembered every detail of that morning.

Her mother in her nightgown, the red velvet one – her best, for when she had to go to hospital or when visiting her children – in the still almost dark *portego*, and her brother Carlo, the lawyer, and head of the family since their father died twenty years before that day.

Was it since that death, since then, that she was like this?

No, there had been wonderful days, of light, of pure joy, even with the war, nights of fear and hope.

No, it happened later, much later, but when? She could not pinpoint the exact moment of her undoing, when she fell apart, when was that?

That morning, there was her brother, still with his coat on and smelling of coffee, and her mother – that purple red blotch in the shadows – who did not look at her but told her to hurry, to get dressed, that she would catch cold in her nightie.

And there were three men dressed in white, by the front door. She could detect the smell of those strangers. She could detect the smell of everything and everybody; before any word, any gesture, before seeing it in their eyes, it was the smell that told her to have confidence or run away, to speak or remain silent or cry out. She immediately detected a hint of sharpness in those three, like a stiletto blade in her brain, an olfactory warning of extreme danger, and so she screamed. She yelled at them to go away, they reeked, who were they, why had they come? And while her mouth emitted the inarticulate sounds that she strove to connect with the meaning of words that were clear in her head, her legs carried her to safety, towards the sanctuary she almost never left: her bedroom.

But she failed to reach it; before she could lock herself in her room, Carlo sprang out and obstructed her, pinning her shoulders to one of the door panels. He stared into her eyes and crushed her with all his weight to prevent her from moving her hands. Then the other three, the men in white, came over and picked her up, carried her to the middle of the *portego* and before her mother's eyes undressed her, put her in a grey jacket with long sleeves, so long that her hands were imprisoned inside them, trapped in the stiff fabric, and then tied behind her back.

She was still screaming when they laid her on a stretcher – Carlo had thrown his coat on it – and carried her out.

Campiello delle Gatte was still deserted at that hour, enshrouded in the milky fog of an autumn dawn, her voice sounded distantly in her ears, as if her cries were those of someone else.

As soon as she felt the air on her face, like a damp and

chilly caress, like the hands of her mother, she calmed down and let them do what they wanted with her.

They put her on to a boat tied up at the waterfront below the house; one of the three men came with her, inside the covered cabin. He did not have that smell of danger, he spoke to her quietly, stroked her forehead.

The rest of those ten years were befuddled with sleep; she slept, she ate, she slept.

And when she woke, the pain in her head wakened too. Then she would go to the window, rest her face against the grille and, if it was night, keep silent, listening to the little sounds of darkness: the rhythmic outpourings of the night birds in the park, the soft lapping of the Lagoon against the island's boat-landing, the wind – when there was any – channelled down the avenue between the branches of the big linden trees. When these were in flower their scent, heightened by the night dampness, loosened every knot and Maria went back to sleep almost with a smile.

But if it was daytime, if the reflection of the water amplified the light and everything before her black-grilled field of vision stood out in greater relief, every smallest detail, the boats in the Santo Spirito canal, the tops of the maritime pines at Sant' Elena, the Ospedale delle Grazie roof tiles, across the water, every particular drove through the solid mass of the vice-like pain in her head like a nail.

Then she screamed and screamed, until a nurse quietened her down with an injection.

Yet she was not uncomfortable in that big and in its own way handsome room, with nothing but the bed, a chair and a white cupboard where her brother had put the linen brought from home, with that scent they used for keeping things fresh, lavender and camomile combined. Whenever she missed her mother, she would open the cupboard and breathe in the smell. Her mother never came, but Carlo and her other brother, Emilio, would come and visit every last Sunday of the month, and bring her mandarine-flavoured ice-cream and one or two new books, usually in French but also in Italian.

She had not forgotten her French, in fact she felt she could speak it better than before, only she had no one she could converse with in French, there on San Clemente, so she would read out loud, when her head expanded a bit allowing her room to say the words.

She kept to her room, a single room her brother the lawyer had obtained for her with difficulty, so she could be alone and not see the horror, not smell the acrid stench of dirt and pain of the other patients. But it was that window that tormented her: she could not help but see it and if she saw it, as if hypnotised, she had to go over to the grille and look out.

And her thoughts became more confused, she could not remember the beginning, nor with any clarity the end; she did, however, remember Bruno's silent love, his bitter smell, his soft beard against her cheeks, his rough hands, the weight of his body on the creaking camp-bed, the flakes of tobacco on the pillow, the anti-aircraft sirens, distant explosions, bright flares to the west, as Marghera and Mestre were bombed.

These were moments of total happiness that came back to her: just the two of them, above a world in ruins, she and that angry and taciturn young man, whom she had got to know at Ca' Foscari.

They would meet on the roof terrace of a palazzo where

one of his former schoolmates lived – the palazzo was practically uninhabited, the family dispersed, with only a deaf old seamstress, who was alone in the world, living on the first floor. Maria would join Bruno there after class – they went separately, being a little more discreet, he said, to protect her from gossip – and they would stay together all afternoon. She made no demands, all she wanted was that suspended time, with no before or after, which within a few months had become the sole purpose of her days. To the young man, her peculiarities, her obsession with smells, with the glances of passers-by, the anxiety that would suddenly seize her and take her breath away, seemed nothing but signs of fear of what surrounded them: war, violence, hunger.

Maria had soon discovered, from their very first encounters, that Bruno was hiding secrets, perhaps a double life: he kept a pistol at the bottom of the little suitcase under his bed, he went out mostly at night, he met people whose names he never mentioned, and he never went home to his parents, who lived somewhere in the province of Padova.

Without being asked, she began to help him, with little things at first: she brought him clean linen, which she washed at home, hiding it from her mother; she filched supplies from the pantry so that he could eat something other than the bread and cheese of which she would find the remains on the table. Then she began doing the other things, things that, albeit reluctantly, Bruno eventually asked her to do: she delivered messages, took food to people she did not know. She ended up distributing leaflets outside schools and the station, and one evening in March she acted as a lookout with him, pretending they were a couple in love – but it was no pretence, they were in love with each other – outside the Goldoni Theatre, while a group of companions interrupted the performance to announce that liberation from the Fascists was imminent.

In other words, without even realising it Maria had become a partisan.

This went on for less than a year.

Bruno disappeared after a round-up, she was arrested at home one morning in August.

It was 1944, though behind the bars on the window of the San Clemente asylum Maria did not remember the date; however, she remembered very well the suffocating heat of that morning, her mother's cries, the nauseating odour on her wrists that smelled of iron and the sweat of others who had worn those same handcuffs, that smell that stayed with her much longer than the month she spent in prison on the Giudecca, the same smell she vaguely detected now from the metal bars on the windows.

Having returned home, she stopped speaking. For years she waited for a sign, a letter from Bruno. Then she stopped waiting.

When the pain was more bearable, when the psychiatric therapies became less harsh and the effect of the electroshock treatment was attenuated, resulting in a less profound lethargy, Maria would leave her room to go to church. She did not pray, she no longer knew the words, she now knew nothing of God or the saints. She would walk through the nave of the almost empty church, and come to a halt before the white marble statue of a semi-nude young man with a great curly beard, bowed under the effort of bearing on his shoulders the enormous weight of a sarcophagus. She would stand in front of that sculpture for hours, for as long as her legs supported her or until an orderly came to fetch her; then she would meekly follow him to her room, where the window of memory awaited her.

But when that redemptive muffling mantle of white fog shrouded the Lagoon, then Maria lost all reference points, she could not see the little bit of City skyline across the water, she remembered nothing, and she surrendered herself to a blessed obliviousness of the small echo of her voice uttering the soft guttural sounds of words she no longer understood.

Perhaps there really was a Maria, who had been in the Resistance, and was an inmate of the provincial asylum of San Clemente, but even if she did not exist, there were certainly others like her, lost behind those walls, of whom we have no record.

Of those walls that once encompassed so much suffering there remains to this day the solid structure built by the Austrians in the mid nineteenth century as an asylum for mentally ill women who had previously been accommodated along with the men in San Servolo – that other island of desolation nearby; as Pompeo Molmenti dolefully comments: *"Echoing their cries* (those of the inmates of San Clemente) *in lugubrious reply are those of the lunatics of San Servolo across the water."*

In its long history the island of San Clemente has been a hostel for pilgrims on their way to the Holy Land, then a convent, then later still an exclusive lazaretto where aristocratic foreigners arriving from places stricken by the plague had to be quarantined. Indeed, it was from San Clemente that the terrible plague of 1630 spread, causing the deaths of 47,000 people in sixteen months – the plague with which the votive church of Madonna della Salute is associated. The chronicles record that on the eighth of June of that year the Marchese di Strigis, sent as an envoy by the Duke of Nevers with rich gifts for the Emperor Ferdinand II, was quarantined on San Clemente with a retinue of five servants: after two days, the marchese fell ill with the plague, passing on the contagion to the unsuspecting carpenter Matteo Tininello, who worked on the island and by returning home to the parish of Sant' Agnese spread the disease.

On lovely San Clemente today, a luxury hotel offers tourists windows without bars, looking out over its magnificent grounds and the pleasing expanse of the southern Lagoon, a real oasis of regenerated verdancy. Fortunately, nothing in its new look gives any intimation of its story of suffering: a welcome and discerning restyling restores for visitors its serenity and beauty.

On the splendid facade of the church dating from the seventeenth century but with Renaissance features, we can read some glorious pages of Venetian history in the still well-preserved bas reliefs. The church was rebuilt on the site of its fifteenth-century predecessor at the behest of Bernardo Morosini, in memory of his father Francesco and brother Tommaso, who died heroically during the Cretan War. Nothing remains of the big canvases and altarpieces; but still there are the inlaid stalls of the choir and the curious reconstruction in polychrome marble of the "House of Loreto", in the apse. And if we venture further into the stark elegance of the interior, we, too, like Maria, can be captivated by that marble figure of a fine bearded man, in a pose of noble suffering, supporting the weight of the epistyle of the monumental tomb of Giorgio Morosini, who died in defence of the freedom and honour of a city by then already destined to fall.

The captivating telamon is the work of the Flemish sculptor Giusto Le Court, author of the Morosini sepulchral monument. And by one of those coincidences or happenstances, a red thread of fate relating to the tragic epidemic that broke out on the island of San Clemente links this sculpture to the votive temple erected by the citizenry to celebrate the ending of the plague. The same Giusto Le Court is also the masterful creator of the high altar of the basilica of Madonna della Salute, that sculptural group in which the Plague, in the terrifying guise of an old woman fleeing from an adorable naked putto armed with a kind of little mop, can be seen – for Venetian children, this was the main reason (certainly it was mine) for going to a votive mass of thanksgiving in the Baroque church behind the Punta della Dogana on the twenty-first of November – beneath the mantle of a huge Madonna and child; the Madonna takes no notice of the scene to her left, turning her benevolent face to the right, towards a bejewelled woman on her knees, praying: a representation of Venice, with a doge's hat lying on a cushion at the feet of the group.

SAN MICHELE

San Michele is without doubt the island in the Lagoon with the greatest number of permanent residents.

It has to be said, these inhabitants would not be able, like a great number of Venetian-born citizens over the past forty years, to decide to move to the mainland. San Michele is their final home, for their mortal remains at least. But within the bounds of its particular nature, the island of San Michele is truly the best place in which to find reconciliation with life, sheltered from the prevailing winds in that open stretch of the Lagoon by a high boundary wall and tranquilly surrounded by expanses of ruffled water festooned with long lines of *bricole* (navigable-channel markers and mooring posts in the Venetian

Lagoon), like sparse winter hedges, in the Venetians' Elysian fields, lovingly tended by the living.

In the end, those who were carried off early
no longer need us,
they are weaned from earth's sorrows and joys, as gently as
children outgrow the soft breasts of their mothers.
But we, who do need such great mysteries,
we for whom
grief is so often the source of our spirit's growth:
could we exist without them?

(Rainer Maria Rilke, *Duino Elegies, The First Elegy* lines 86-91, trans. Stephen Mitchell)

So, serenely mindful, indeed hopeful, of in due course becoming one with the earth within those pink walls topped with white stone from Brac, let us delve into the story of San Michele.

What we see today is the result of the nineteenth-century unifying of two islands, San Michele, so close to Murano that it was used as a *cavana* for sheltering boats that plied the northern route, and the nearby small island of San Cristoforo della Pace, looking towards the north face of the City, the long and extremely windswept walkway of the Fondamente Nove.

The ground allocated by Napoleonic edict to accommodate deceased citizens – whether of the nobility or the common folk – of the subjugated Republic was initially limited to the island of San Cristoforo, a place with a worthy past but rather different from that of being ground consecrated to eternal peace. Let us say that its role was always associated with peace, though not of the soul but the senses, with the construction of a hostel dedicated to Saints Cristoforo and Onofrio that took in so-called "fallen women". The hostel was short-lived. It is not recorded in the chronicles whether it ceased to fulfil its function because of a lack of raw material, in other words the demise of such waywardness and a general redemption, or, more probably, because of the limited appeal of the hostel to the category of its potential clients. What is certain is that the said hostel lost its funding and, inevitably, its redemptive work came to an end.

After a much repeated turnover of monastic orders that succeeded each other on the little island, the Austin friars established themselves there, under the canonship of Fra' Simone da Camerino, who had the great merit of acting as a peace negotiator between the Republic and the Duke of Milan, Francesco Sforza, leading to the epithet "della Pace" being added to the name of the ferryman early saint, the time-honoured eponymous patron of our island.

From engravings of views that have come down to us we can deduce that the Augustinians enjoyed generous funding, since the church, built by Pietro Lombardo, and the adjoining monastery buildings, designed with architectural restraint, were of considerable size. When Napoleon – who, as Ivone Cacciavillani notes, was never referred to by name in popular historiography but simply as "I", alluding to the title of *Imperatore* (Emperor) but also implying the qualifying term *"Infame"* (Villain) – saw fit to dismantle churches and convents, the buildings on San Cristoforo were also demolished, but not before the friars had joined the splendid monastery of San

Stefano within the City. Plans were drawn up, in compliance with the sanitary provisions of the edict of Saint-Cloud, for a new cemetery for the citizens of Venice to be built on the ruins of the San Cristoforo monastery, and the project was entrusted to Giannantonio Selva, the celebrity architect of that period, who had designed the pageant in welcome of the arrival of "I", and who was able to include in his professional resumé the Teatro La Fenice, and the theatres in Trieste and Feltre, and not least his close and warm friendship with the godlike and powerful Canova.

But as also happens today with celebrity architects, between the conception of a grand project and its realisation flows a river of money that in those, as in these, murky years of pillage dried up, leaving the City coffers drought-stricken. So much so that the ambitious plan was scaled down and converted into the construction of a more modest boundary wall of brick and an octagonal chapel. Meanwhile, the graveyard was raised by a couple of metres, to place it beyond the reach of the tides, using soil dredged from the canal. But this recycled soil, being clay-rich, soon proved to be the least suitable for interment and consequently that holy ground turned out before long to be insufficient, and to fulfil that pious need the choice fell on nearby San Michele, separated from San Cristoforo by a canal that in 1835 was filled in, and which thereby became the natural extension of the original City cemetery.

Since the beginning of its history there had been on this second island a small church, little more than a chapel, dedicated to the archangel Michael; and it so happens that the extreme desolation of the place offered the appropriate refuge to Romualdo, a Benedictine monk of noble origin from Ravenna, seeking the isolation conducive to meditation and prayer. It was this very same Romualdo who had the great distinction of persuading Doge Orseolo I to abandon the Palazzo Ducale in great haste – without even a word to his family – leaving behind an ugly situation in international politics, to become a hermit himself, but far from the Lagoon, in a remote monastery in the Pyrenees mountains, then under Catalan control, Saint-Michel de Cuxa, a stronghold of the powerful abbot Guarino, where the former doge – later saint – died in an odour of sanctity and where a very modest unembellished stone to this day marks his peaceful passing. As for Romualdo, having carried out this mission, he completed his arduous progress towards sainthood, among his innumerable other merits founding the Camaldolese monastic order.

And in fact the Camaldolese established themselves on the island of San Michele, after it was granted to them by the bishops of Torcello and Olivolo in 1212; there the good monks strove so hard to increase its prestige that after a few decades the San Michele establishment was promoted to the status of abbey. This golden period for San Michele coincided with the second half of the fifteenth century, when the construction of the monastery took place under the direction of the great Lombardi, after whom came the brilliant Mauro Codussi and the building of the church, the most beautiful example of Renaissance architecture in the Lagoon; to which, the white casket of the Cappella Emiliana, extending towards the water, built by Guglielmo Bergamasco and commissioned by Margherita Vitturi, widow of Giovan Battista Emiliani, is a worthy appendage.

This was a period of exceptional vitality for the monastic

community, which prospered on San Michele, giving rise to the most important and productive Venetian scriptorium.

In the quiet of the scriptorium, within its pale-green painted walls – this restful colour being the most favourable to concentration, attuned to the liquid hues of its sacred Lagoon confines – the monks were responsible for producing codices of rare quality and variety. And located within those same walls from 1430 was the cartographic workshop of Fra Mauro, the great cosmographer who, in collaboration with Andrea Bianco, created the amazing mappa mundi conserved in the Biblioteca Marciana.

Added to such ingenuity and expertise was the zeal of the abbot Pietro Dolfin, who in bringing together scribes, copyists, scholars and men of letters gave great impetus to the library and to its collection of manuscripts. The library continued over the following centuries to increase its literary treasure trove until in 1810 the monks had to abandon the island, moving to San Gregorio al Celio in Rome, taking with them their extraordinary patrimony of some 180,000 volumes and 36,000 codices, in addition to their extremely precious archive.

Meanwhile the cemetery began to fulfil its own hallowed function of offering eternal repose to wretched humanity, which as we know is dust and to dust it will return. But mightier than Time and human fate, on the quiet sequestered shelves of the library of San Michele, in stalwart alliance, indomitable ink and paper endured.

And it was from that library, a few years ago and thanks to the scholar Angela Nuovo, there came the solution to a mystery that had vexed and intrigued the most erudite bibliophiles in the world.

The story begins in 1537, in the City, world centre of culture and publishing, where the inimitable Manutius had invented the modern book.

After the great Aldus' death in 1515, another family of printers, the Paganini, originally from Brescia, operated as publishers with great success, producing books of exceptional quality and typographical complexity. Specialising in texts of a religious nature, Paganino Paganini and his son Alessandro had published the three very complicated mathematical books of Luca Pacioli. Combining business acumen with a talent for printing, these two Brescian-Venetians had perceived the potential expansion of the book market well beyond the bounds – extensive though these were – of Europe.

Thanks to the close relationship between Paganino and Giovanni Bartolomeo Gabiano – they had married two sisters, the daughters of a renowned German printer with a workshop at Rialto under the sign of the Fountain – and with the benefit of Gabiano's contacts in Constantinople through a Serbian relative who was very well connected with the Ottoman court, an extremely ambitious plan evolved for the Paganini press to produce a printed edition of the Koran in Arabic. The enterprise promised to be extremely lucrative: the Islamic people did not yet have the equipment for typographic printing and the holy book was transcribed by hand, with very limited circulation.

So before the Paganini's eyes opened up the prospect of satisfying the enormous absorption capacity in the Turco-Arabic market; at that time no one in the West had the interest or the competence to read an edition of the Koran entirely in Arabic. But the difficulties of typographic transcription of the Arabic characters, whose form varies according to their position in the word – it has been calculated that the Paganini had recourse to matrices for around six hundred different "sorts" – led to the final result being unsatisfactory. With an abundance of errors, such that they distorted the text, the Venetian Koran of 1538 proved to be a total failure. In 1588 the French Humanist Jean Bodin reported the condemnation to death in Constantinople of a Venetian merchant who had imported a printed Koran offensive for its errors and consequent mystifications, all copies of which were destroyed. Through the intercession of La Serenissima's *bailo* (diplomatic representative) at the Ottoman court the death sentence was commuted to the amputation of the imprudent Venetian merchant's right hand. It is to be noted that no official news of what happened on the Bosphorus ever reached the Signoria, which was otherwise constantly kept informed through prolific correspondence with its ambassadors in the extremely delicate seat of the former Second Rome. Further news, dating from some forty years later, regarding the fate of the ghostly Paganini Koran is to be found in the writings of Thomas Erpenius, the greatest Orientalist of that time, who asserted: of the Paganini Koran *"omnia exemplaria cremata sunt"* (all examples are cremated).

Over the centuries there has been conjecture as to what became of the Paganini Koran, with the suspicion that the burning was attributable to papal decree, or more likely to the decision of the printer himself to destroy the disastrous result of such an ambitious project.

Whatever the truth of it, all traces of the Venetian Koran were lost and also any hope of getting to the bottom of the mystery, so much so that there was even doubt as to whether it actually existed, with the supposition that the proof version never got published.

In 1987 among the holdings of the San Michele library, Angela Nuovo, a sixteenth-century specialist and researcher into the Paganini press, came across a 232-leaf volume that had once belonged to the scholar and polyglot Teseo Ambrogio degli Albonesi and had been acquired by the island's library by one of those mysterious and fascinating routes that a book sometimes takes, surviving time's wear and tear and the short-sighted rejection of human beings.

The rediscovery, despite its being destined for burning, of the sole surviving copy of the Koran printed in movable type in Arabic as a result of the Paganinis' ill-fated commercial far-sightedness, solved what had been a mystery for many centuries.

That book, rescued from oblivion, is now conserved in the monastic library of San Francesco della Vigna, a few hundred metres distant from its original, unknowing safe-haven, across the briny water, on the sacred soil of San Michele in Isola, from which we citizens of the unnameable ravaged marvel may perhaps rise again, but from which an exemplary product of its prodigious mercantile and artistic culture has certainly been resurrected.

THE ANGEL OF SAN GIORGIO MAGGIORE

It was a November afternoon and it had been a warm, soft day of hazy sunshine.

The City at peace sprawled lazily, as it can when it wants to, its stones, relieved at last of footfall, relaxing into the white edging blocks on the waterfront, grey fingers with long white nails.

The canals, constricted within their brick boundaries, the red substratum of the palazzi, sought, by slowly raising the surface, an equilibrium for their deeper fast-running water clearly under pressure from a new influx.

Higher up, above the top floors of the crooked facades, not a breath of air stirred.

The air was as if trapped by the spumy film of dampness rising from the canal to the stones and from the stones to the tiles and from the tiles to the low patch of sky above the City.

A pleasant mellowness, an unseasonably warm day.

On a day like this it was possible, then, to enjoy this glorious City in holiday mood, conscious of the privilege, with freedom of movement, without having to slip down secret back alleys, hugging the walls and cursing. Adolescent-like, to be new to the place, to discover unexpected details in the familiar, to have a willingness to be surprised, enchanted and then to wander back home following some suggestion, a smell, the colour of the stucco facades reacting to the humidity.

I happened, almost unintentionally, to emerge from Campo di San Zaccaria, the church more rosy than ever in the brief interlude of sunset, and to walk across the waterfront to the unusually deserted boat stop for the number one ferry, the slow, contemplative holiday ride. The *flaneurs'* ride.

From the as yet unlighted landing-stage – it must have been about four o'clock, but already it was steeped in shadow – I saw the church tower of San Giorgio before me disappear, starting at the top, quickly swallowed up in a thick cottony fog. As if a hand wielding a giant paintbrush had, with an artist's rapid stroke, painted white first the green roof, then the black-perforated belfry, the reddish shaft, then the base, obliterating in no time, perhaps a couple of minutes, the island of San Giorgio Maggiore itself.

Leaving nothing, nothing other than the small, salted, opaque panes of the still-deserted floating landing-stage.

Meanwhile, from the left, from the stretch of water separating the Lagoon-side of Riva degli Schiavoni from the island that had just been obliterated, approaches the squat-shaped prow of the ferry-boat, clearly visible, familiar.

It ties up, people get off, I get on.

I stand on the open deck; it is a short hop to the Punta della Salute. That is where I have planned to spend the last part of the day, a place for lovers, where youngsters playing truant spend the morning, a place of existential melancholy, of subtle joy, of breezes.

The boat sets off, directing its prow eastwards, and swinging out into the open, away from that busy node of water traffic along the quayside in front of San Marco.

But that white paintbrush, that fog over San Giorgio, within a moment, had already enveloped the basin, transforming it into a void, emptied of people, objects, buildings, domes and waterfronts. A basinful of nothing, a container of milk in the encroaching darkness.

There were few passengers who had stayed out on the deck with me: standing in silence, each of us thinking our own thoughts, like figures in a Hopper painting, like trees in a landscape.

I still do not know why that boat took such an out-of-the-way route into the Grand Canal, probably some unexpected curtain of fog disorientated the captain.

Denser wafts of mist, like visible puffs of breath, licked the open sides of the vessel that was moving at extremely reduced speed; through the quiet purring of the diesel engine came the muffled sound of a siren, like a stifled cry.

A flash of white light, refracted and immediately absorbed by the milky suspension in water, rips through the void, the opaque foggy darkness.

An enormous black angel appears to me, its wings spread

in flight, motionless, close by, awesome. Quite distinct in the gloom, yet very dark in that sinister whiteness of fog. A few metres away from me, from the side of the boat, for the infinite duration of one moment of total, unreasoning terror.

The oncoming ferry's siren sounded just as its fog light illuminated that apocalyptic vision, which, it seemed, no one but me had observed.

Then the sound too ceased, our boat corrected its course with a sudden swing to starboard, moving over to the right-hand side of the canal.

The few passengers around me, indistinct figures in the gloom, showed no signs of alarm.

The *flaneurs'* boat service continued on its sedate journey, unperturbed.

I was left with the certainty that I had suffered an extraordinary, formidable hallucination. Until the local newspaper a few days later reported the removal and transportation – in challenging circumstances, due to an unexpected and extremely thick blanket of fog – of the huge angel from San Giorgio's bell-tower.

The wooden statue, clad with sheets of copper, was struck by lightning during a terrible storm on 5 September 1993: while the wooden structure was irreparably damaged, the metal cladding, completely darkened by the electrical discharge, was salvageable.

That November late afternoon a barge equipped with an hydraulic-arm crane had lifted the huge angel from the waterside on the island of San Giorgio Maggiore in order to transport it to the conservation laboratory where my terrifying black angel was restored.

POSTSCRIPT

In this map of the Lagoon the uncharted areas are far more extensive than those I have charted – as in the geography of the Lagoon itself, which is almost entirely blue with only small and scattered concentrations of brown-green, like a rarefied, heaven-made *drip painting*. Many of the individuals who appear in these pages are the fruit of my imagination or desire. Mine is just a sketch map, an impression of the Lagoon universe, real and imaginary. But who can say with any certainty how much of what is seen in a reflection is reality and not appearance?

Islands seen and imagined, spits of sand swallowed up by water and regurgitated, mouths with lips of earth open to the sea, grass that becomes algae, purple marine florescences, effuse white pollen transmuted into spume, salt that turns to light, underwater birds and flying fish, water fields and shell gardens, wetlands and rolling hills of mist, liquid lanes, silt pathways, light winds and dark winds, sea breezes and earthy smells, water that regenerates, water that invades, water that cures and contaminates, water that nurtures and teaches, water that is never satisfied, water that devastates, villainous water, innocent water, ever-varying water – the brackish waters of the Lagoon.

Dedalus Celebrating Women's Literature 2018–2028

In 2018 Dedalus began celebrating the centenary of women getting the vote in the UK with a programme of women's fiction. In 1918, Parliament passed an act granting the vote to women over the age of 30 who were householders, the wives of householders, occupiers of property with an annual rent of £5 or graduates of British universities. About 8.4 million women gained the vote. It was a big step forward but it was not until the Equal Franchise Act of 1928 that women over 21 were able to vote and women finally achieved the same voting rights as men. This act increased the number of women eligible to vote to 15 million. Dedalus' aim is to publish 6 titles each year, most of which will be translations from other European languages, for the next 10 years as we commemorate this important milestone.

Titles published so far:

The Prepper Room by Karen Duve
Take Six: Six Portuguese Women Writers edited by Margaret Jull Costa
Slav Sisters: The Dedalus Book of Russian Women's Literature edited by Natasha Perova
Baltic Belles: The Dedalus Book of Estonian Women's Literature edited by Elle-Mari Talivee
The Madwoman of Serrano by Dina Salústio
Cleopatra goes to Prison by Claudia Durastanti

The Price of Dreams by Margherita Giacobino
Primordial Soup by Christine Leunens
The Girl from the Sea and other Stories by Sophia de Mello Breyner Andresen
The Medusa Child by Sylvie Germain
Venice Noir by Isabella Panfido

Forthcoming titles include:

Baltic Belles: The Dedalus Book of Latvian Women's Literature edited by Eva Eglaja
Fair Trade Heroin by Rachael McGill
Chasing the Dream by Liane de Pougy
A Woman's Affair by Liane de Pougy
Co-Wives, Co-Widows by Adrienne Yabouza
Catalogue of a Private Life by Najwa Binshatwan
Eddo's Souls by Stella Gaitano

> For further information please contact Dedalus at
> info@dedalusbooks.com

Recommended Reading

If you have enjoyed reading *Venice Noir* you should enjoy the other City Noir titles in the series:

Paris Noir by Jacques Yonnet
Prague Noir by Sylvie German

If you like books about Italy by Italian authors you should try:

Portrait of a Family with a Fat Daughter by Margherita Giacobino
The Mussolini Canal by Antonio Pennacchi
Cleopatra goes to Prison by Claudia Durastanti
God's Dog by Diego Marani
I Malavoglia by Giovanni Verga
The Late Mattia Pascal by Luigi Pirandello

If you want to read more books by women authors with a fantasy element you should try:

The Prepper Room by Karen Duve
The Book of Nights by Sylvie Germain
The Medusa Child by Sylvie Germain
Primordial Soup by Christine Leunens
Light-Headed by Olga Slavnikova

These books can be bought from your local bookshop or online from your favourite internet bookseller or direct from Dedalus. Please write to Cash Sales, Dedalus Limited, 24-26 St Judith's Lane, Sawtry, Cambs, PE28 5XE. For further details of the Dedalus list please go to our website www.dedalusbooks.com

Paris Noir – Jacques Yonnet

'Concentrating on the seedy area around Rue Mouffetard, which becomes "La Mouffe" in a typically Parisian abbreviation, Yonnet reveals the dark side of the City of Light in the 1940s in this "secret history of a city". The street life of the Left Bank ticks on much as normal during the Occupation, though Léopoldie the tart stops turning tricks because "the green German uniform does not suit her complexion". Keep-on-Dancin', the killer with a fondness for history, rules the roost. Though describing himself as "sceptical, disillusioned, cynical", Yonnet casually dispatches a traitor in the Resistance. This is film noir in book form.'

Christopher Hirst in *The Independent*

'Yonnet evokes a wonderful and frightening world that lurks in the dark interstices of the City of Light: beggars, whores and poets, people who are quick to draw a knife or cast a spell, and are completely foreign to notions of "responsible" drinking and sexual behaviour. The Old Man Who Appears After Midnight, Tricksy-Pierrot, the Watchmaker of Backward-Running Time and many others haunt a warren of streets and stews where supernatural events are frequent: a vicious one-eyed ginger tom is reincarnated as a murderous lover; a gypsy curse putrefies a hostile hostelry. What makes Yonnet's memoir so special is the way the real and fantastic meet. After all, it is set during the Occupation, and the author was a Resistance hero. The secrets of Paris play a role in the struggle against the Germans and their collaborators. Thus, the occultist spiv

Keep-on-Dancin' initiates Yonnet to a "psychic circuit" that enables him to unmask a Gestapo informer in "the room where only the truth can be told". Yonnet portrays Paris as a character in her own right: the city is "edgy", the Seine "sulks". The geography determines the behaviour of its inhabitants, and will live on after their deaths. Certain névralgique points in the city incite Parisians to raise barricades, be it during revolutions or the Liberation of 1944.'   Gavin Bond in *Scotland on Sunday*

'Like Christopher Isherwood's 1939 novel *Goodbye to Berlin*, this book sidelines conventional history in favour of anecdotal, autobiographical and brilliantly subjective snapshots of the city's marginalised "human detritus" in a series of cinematic vignettes that straddle the real, the absurd and the supernatural.'   Alex Barlow in *Time Out*

'In 1940 young Jacques Yonnet, escaping the Nazis took refuge in Paris, his destination the part of the city that few knew intimately, the dark underbelly of the Left Bank where tramps, artists, criminals and con men lived in close and colourful proximity. Focusing both on the city's history between the wars and on the years under occupation, his atmospheric, bewitching account is an evocative slice of non-fiction that defies easy categorization: a beguiling narrative where mystery seeps through every page.'
The Good Book Guide

£9.99 ISBN 978 1 903517 48 2 280p B. Format

Prague Noir (The Weeping Woman on the Streets of Prague) – Sylvie Germain

'An intricate, finely crafted and polished tale, *The Weeping Woman* brings magic-realism to the dimly lit streets of Prague. Through the squares and alleys a woman walks, the embodiment of human pity, sorrow, death. Everyone she passes is touched by her, and Germain skilfully creates an intense mood and feel in her attempt to produce a spiritual map of Prague.'
The Observer

'Firmly rooted in magic realism, Germain adds her own strain of dark romanticism and macabre imagination to create a tale poised between vision and elegy.'

Emily Dean in *The Sunday Times*

'Hallucinatory, lyrical in the extreme, it's a post-modernist playground for literary game-playing. It seems, at first, a radical departure for this gifted tale-teller but no, this is a teasing meditation on her familiar themes: history, place, creativity, death and desire.' James Friel in *Time Out*

'The figure of this bereft woman develops into a memorable symbol: her sudden appearances – on a bridge, in a square, in a room – haunt the book like history, moved to tears.'

Robert Winder in *The Independent*

£8.99   ISBN 978 1 903517 73 4   112p   B. Format

Portrait of a Family with a Fat Daughter – Margherita Giacobino

'This memoir of four generations of a family provides a vivid and eloquent picture of Italian life stretching from the late 19th century, when the peasant lifestyle had changed little from medieval times, up to the consumer culture of the 1950s. In writing about her female-dominated family, some of whom she is old enough to remember – most notably the matriarchal grandmother Ninin – Giacobino imbues her account with a real sense of intimacy. She has a powerful feel for traditional Italian culture, her early chapters conjuring up a time when the hierarchy of the family was the only true reality, fairness was unknown and "a moment's tenderness must last a week".'
Alastair Mabbutt in *The Herald*

'It's like a rural version of Elena Ferrante's Neapolitan saga. A powerful and atmospheric record of largely unexplored terrain.' Margaret Drabble in *The Times Literary Supplement*

'This sweeping narrative explores what it means to be Italian across oceans and historical epochs. Its vivid descriptions and deep cultural understanding leave a lasting mark.'
Italian Prose Award 2019 shortlist

£12.99 ISBN 978 1 910213 48 3 304p B. Format

The Mussolini Canal – Antonio Pennacchi

'Antonio Pennacchi's boldly engaging novel could be read as a graphic social history. It is this to some extent but it is also lively and funny. *The Mussolini Canal* is an earthy story of underlining seriousness told with a gruff bluster of a narrator possessed of an astonishing grasp of his family's story – which also happens to be that of his country… There are obvious echoes of *One Hundred Years of Solitude* and *The Grapes of Wrath* and even slight hints of *The Tin Drum*, but most of all Pennacchi's large-hearted narrative balances the domestic with the international. As the narrator announces: "Heed me I have a story to tell." And he certainly does.'

Eileen Battersby in *The Irish Times*

'…the story itself is utterly compelling… *The Mussolini Canal*, the winner of the Strega Prize, Italy's most prestigious literary award, in 2010, is surely Pennacchi's masterwork, written with a rare feel for the present-day idiom across memory, nostalgic but sardonically so. Judith Landry's translation hits the mark every time… It's a big, generous read, a historical giro with stamina and heart.'

Brian Morton's Novel of The Week in *The Tablet*

'My favourite novel of the year, it is a sweeping, giddying tale of those impoverished northern Italians who were relocated in the 1930s to farm the area of former swampland south of Rome, many of whom became ardent fascists. An exquisitely composed work of political and social insight, it is as humorous as it is haunting.'

Rosemary Goring in *The Herald's Books of the Year*

'*The Mussolini Canal* by Antonio Pennacchi is an epic account of the rise of Fascism. It's the story of the (fictitious) Peruzzi clan of sharecroppers, moved from their native north to the malaria-ridden Pontine Marshes for the building of the canal and the New Town of Littoria. It mingles family legend and up-to-date political commentary with personal appearances from Edmondo Rossoni and Mussolini, and takes us through Italy's Imperium and the campaign in Ethiopia to the Anzio landings. The complex chronology and the demotic and combative narrative voice (of a young Peruzzi descendant) are imaginatively handled by the translator, Judith Landry, and the novel presents us with a whole new landscape, complete with the kiwi fruits and eucalyptus that thrived in the reclaimed land. Better than any guidebook, it explains how and at what cost Mussolini succeeded where Romans, popes and emperors failed. A challenging but very illuminating read.'

Margaret Drabble's Books of the Year in
The Times Literary Supplement

'...his glorious mishmash of a peasant's eye view of the first half of 20th century Italy deservedly won the Strega Prize. A book of many layers, beneath the history, political commentary, and humour, it is a novel about the strength of the family. right or wrong, they stick together and that is how they survive. Credit must go to the translator Judith Landry, for capturing the spirit of the work. A spectacular work of earthy humour.'

Scarlet McGuire in *Tribune*

£12.99   ISBN 978 1 909232 24 2   536p   B. Format

I Malavoglia – Giovanni Verga

'Giovanni Verga's novel of 1881 *I Malavoglia* presented its translator Judith Landry with formidable problems of dialect and peasant speech which she has solved so unobtrusively that one wonders why this moving and tragic tale is so little known in England.'

Margaret Drabble in *The Observer's Books of the Year*

'Written in 1881 and set in the Sicilian village of Aci Trezza in the 1860s, Verga's novel charts the failing fortunes of the Malavoglia, a family of fisherfolk who are living through a period of political change following the country's annexation to Italy. The Malavoglias' inexorable slide is triggered by the decision of Padron 'Ntoni to buy a cargo of lupins on credit after a bad year of business, only to lose the precious cargo in a storm at sea. The repayment of this debt leads to the loss of the family home, and all subsequent efforts to reclaim it are doomed. The old values are dying and it is largely due to young 'Ntoni, exposed to the outside world during naval service and ever more dissatisfied by the life endured by the rest of Aci Trezza's charmingly loquacious inhabitants, that the family fortunes are never restored. A tragic account of the sort of disquiet visited upon a family by the vague desire for the unknown, their struggle for survival is depicted by Verga with stark honesty.'

Anna Scott in *The Guardian*

'This is a tragic tale of poverty, honour and survival in a society where the weak go to the wall unmourned.'

The Sunday Times

£9.99   ISBN 978 1 910213 23 0   268p   B. Format